Just Beneath

the Surface

D1444539

By Keri A. Kovacsiss
and Lea M. Kovacsiss

Just Beneath the Surface

By Keri A. Kovacsiss and Lea M. Kovacsiss
Copyright © 2022 Keri A. Kovacsiss and Lea
M. Kovacsiss

Cover design: Pace Studios
ISBN:979-8-9866326-0-5

Dedication

This book is dedicated to sisters, biological or chosen: there is nothing more powerful on this earth than our bond.

Contents

Acknowledgments

First and foremost, we would like to thank Ryan McAuley, our incredible parents, Bob and Tami Kovacsiss, grandmother, Patricia Kovacsiss, sister, Jamie Ickes, and larger family. This project would not be a reality without your constant support and encouragement. To our editors Mark Hanigan and Jenny Spencer: we can't thank you enough for your tireless work on this project or for putting up with us. To Amanda Riley: thank you for the countless hours that you put in on this project, reviewing and teaching us some modicum of social media literacy. We hope that you have hair left on your head after teaching us hashtags. To Maria Licodo Pace: thank you for your enthusiasm and for translating our vision into a physical medium and book description.

Chapter 1

Autumn is the best time of year in Seven Hills with orange and brown leaves on the ground, pumpkins on porches, and skeletons in the windows. One of the things that I love about Seven Hills is the way residents always adorn their homes with paper decorations, reluctant to buy the flashy, light-up, monstrosities offered at Value Mart. Not only because Value Mart was more than a 20-minute drive away from Seven Hills, but because Halloween was sacred.

The townsfolk of Seven Hills spent more time and energy on Halloween than Christmas. The build-up to the holiday began in late August. During this time, the weather was still warm, but there was a bit of a chill in the air, making everything crisp. Despite the last of the summer heat struggling to hang on, the town would turn itself over. Bright pink flamingos and tiny swimming pools were removed from lawns, and pumpkins would begin to appear, already carved on porches. Bright autumn wreathes would be hung on doors. Without exception, every business created elaborate Halloween displays in their windows, often based upon a theme.

One business would create a spectacular Dracula-themed display worthy of a magazine spread. Another would create a fall wonderland covered with leaves, pinecones, and twinkling lights. The local theatre, lovingly decorated to the hilt with pumpkins, hay bales, skeletons, and faux spider webs, would begin playing spooky movies. Everyone rushed to the theatre to enjoy *A Nightmare on Elm Street*, *Halloween*, and *Hocus Pocus* over fistfuls of buttery popcorn and chocolate candy. There was nothing like watching a classic horror film on the big screen. My sisters and I would drive to watch a scary movie weekly in the fall. All of us would pile into my older sister Theodora's station wagon, with thick, plaid blankets wrapped around our knees. On the way home, we would be so scared that the familiar winding roads back to our family home would seem creepy and strange.

For the residents of Seven Hills, loving Halloween, and all things supernatural, is in their blood. Seven Hills, which is close to Salem, Massachusetts, is a popular tourist destination, as there were witches tried and hanged in the town's square in 1693. A total of five women were accused and convicted of practicing Witchcraft. All five women, all beautiful, were rumored to be members of a powerful coven that 'took the manhood' of men in the town in order to achieve power. Now, the common narrative and understanding of the hangings was that the women, refusing to marry the men, were accused of practicing Witchcraft as revenge.

Despite the horror experienced by these five women, in modern times, they were vindicated. The women are now regarded as heroes in Seven Hills. Each year, they are honored through the town's All Hallows' Eve Parade and subsequent Pageant. At least one parade float, if not more, depicts the history of these five women and the tragic events leading up to their hanging. The five women are lauded as iconic superheroes during the retellings. Tourists and townspersons alike listen with starry eyes to the stories, discussing how brave the women were. In death, all five women had become legends. After the parade each year, all would attend the All Hallows' Eve Pageant, continuing the celebration of female beauty and power. Despite Seven Hills' dark history, the town had turned the plights of these five women into something enchanting, mysterious, and worthy of celebration. Walking through the town during this time of year, you can feel the history and the magic.

I am no stranger to magic, having grown up in the tradition. My mother and her sister, my Aunt Elaina, worked and owned Seven Hills' apothecary shop, The Alchemist. My first memories were spent at The Alchemist. I remember going through the shop, running my hands over the jars of potions, smelling the dried herbs, and even falling asleep on cardboard boxes with my sisters, Theodora and Tara, when it got too late. Our mother, smelling of lavender and sage, would wake us up to tell us it was finally time to go home.

In a way, The Alchemist was an extension of our home, our mother, and our family. In my mind's eye, I could still see her there, bent over a pot, mixing together a variety of ingredients, with the most enticing aroma filling the air. Her dark hair would be falling from her bun and curling up at the sides from the steam. My mother always seemed to be bent over some type of creation. Each one earthy, mysterious, and—and no doubt—potent, three words that I would use to describe her.

She seemed to be plucked out of a different time. Only in this lifetime, she had been burdened with taking care of three little screaming, crying animals; not that she would ever think of us as a burden. Though, she probably did think of us as animals. People, after all, are animals. *All creatures are valuable*, she used to tell us. I have so many fond memories of those times at The Alchemist, with my sisters, my aunt, and my mother.

I had many bad memories from this time as well; memories that gave me nightmares. Sometimes, I would wake up in the middle of the night from anxiety-induced dreams in which the police finally came to get us. In my dreams, I would see their blue and red lights flashing outside of our home and would know what was to come. Panicked, I would search for a place to hide, knowing full well that hiding would be useless. I would awaken drenched in sweat, panting. For a moment, before I was fully conscious and aware, I would forget that I was an adult. I would forget that I was safe. I would worry that my mother was gone. Then, I would remember that, although my childhood fears were never realized, she *was* gone. She would always be gone now, buried in Seven Hills Cemetery, beneath a tombstone that read: *Diana Culpepper, A Beautiful*

4

Mother. A sob would catch in my throat at the thought of her *gone*, a word she would never use. A child never really stops wanting their mother.

Although The Alchemist business went through its ups and downs when I was a child, the overall upward direction remained steady throughout the years. By the time my older sister, Theodora, took complete control of The Alchemist, business was booming. Part of that success was due to Seven Hills becoming an extremely popular tourist destination, and by extension, The Alchemist becoming one as well. Witches are popular now; witches are cool. There is a plethora of mainstream books available on Witchcraft; there seems to be endless Netflix series about the topic as well. Tara, Theo, and I would watch these shows in the living room of our family home, trying to make the antique furniture comfy with plush blankets and pillows. We could buy new furniture. We could buy a lot of new things, but we never did. We enjoyed the witch shows, the books, the novelties. How fun! Witchcraft without consequences; Witchcraft without suspicion.

During the autumn months, people rushed to our shop to buy up souvenirs to bring back to their friends and relatives— perfumes, soaps, makeup, salves, lotions, essential oils, and dried herbs– all homemade. Of course, each item was cleverly packaged as something authentic, rare, and magical. We even sold the occasional love potion—not a 'real' love potion of course. Not that we did not know how to make such a thing, but love potions require quite a bit more than mixing a few ingredients. Love potions and spells require discipline, ritual, and often, bodily fluids. Asking a friendly tourist to get a hold of a potential lover's blood, hair, or even semen was awkward; and I do not imagine that would help business, even if it might help their love lives.

On one of those glorious autumn mornings, I hurried into The Alchemist, stealing sips of my piping-hot coffee, and wrapping my thick, wool sweater around me. It was a perfect morning, chilly but not too cold. I threw open the door, and the sleigh bell rang. I knew Theodora would already be there, opening the register, dusting the shelves, and wiping the windows. She was chronically early, chronically over-achieving, and chronically perfect. Although Seven Hills had become a tourist destination, a big part of the reason for our business's success was Theo. She was a brilliant businesswoman. I suspect she could probably take some college courses, apply, and get hired by a thriving company. She could probably make 100 times what she was making here, but she never would. She is rooted here.

As I walked through the large door, I was greeted by the pleasant aroma of rosemary and sage, infused with the slight smell of coconut oil. There was another scent this morning that was perhaps out of place: freshly baked pumpkin scones. I would know the smell of those pumpkin scones anywhere. Deidra had already been in. Deidra Parker owned the local bakery. The bakery sat catty-corner from The Alchemist, cleverly named Seven Sweets. After years of my sisters and I cajoling her, Deidra, my best friend since childhood, finally gave in and opened a shop where she could sell those delicious treats that she was always making for parties and holidays. Her

treats were especially welcomed this time of the year. Her bright teal counters were stocked with everything from pumpkin cheesecakes to hazelnut brownies to gooey pumpkin caramel bars, dusted with powdered sugar.

Putting down my satchel, I practically tore into the bright teal box, tied with a single white ribbon, to get a pumpkin scone. I don't know why she made this packaging effort for us. She could throw the endless supply of treats she gave us into brown paper bags or old Tupperware containers. I brought this up with her many times; she could save boxes. She would listen quietly and then respond, "I like pageantry." I guess we all liked 'pageantry' in Seven Hills. That must be in our blood as well. I picked up the treat and took a bite. The delicious taste of pumpkin, vanilla, cinnamon, and buttercream frosting melted in my mouth. I took a swig of coffee. *There is truly nothing better*, I thought.

"Well, you and Tara are late, as usual," Theodora said, coming out from the back. Her black hair was twisted into a knot, and she was wearing an old apron.

"Tara is later," I countered, slouching into the large, plaid, wingback chair, that was our favorite sitting destination, and enjoying my scone.

We usually worked separate shifts at The Alchemist, but this week we needed all-hands-on-deck. The All Hallows' Eve Parade, Pageant, and Party were just over one week away. Typically, Theodora worked the early shift, I the next, and then Tara would normally come in for a few hours to finish up the day. This time of the year, however, we all were needed. Between decorations for the festivities and regular orders, there was so much to prepare. To top it all off, soon the street would be thick with tourists. At times, it seems almost impossible to keep products on the shelves.

"Check out what came," Theo said, nodding her head towards an open, cardboard box sitting on a large mahogany table.

I walked over to the box and pulled it open, "Ah, the candle votives! I am so excited! I've been wanting to get started on these. I think the candles will be perfect with the holidays coming up."

I closed my eyes and envisioned all the holiday candles I would make: peppermint, balsam, pumpkin, campfire, cranberry, fir, cocoa, and fresh brewed coffee.

We went about our duties, and eventually Tara showed up. She had on leather pants, an oversized black hoodie, and large black sunglasses.

"Aw, the old hag has arrived," I said.

"Hottest old hag you've ever seen," she said, removing her sunglasses. She revealed perfectly manicured eyelashes and brows beneath her shades.

"Theo is going to kill you," I said, causally. "Want a scone?"

Tara sat down on a wooden chair and grabbed a scone. She then grabbed my coffee and took a couple of swigs. I rolled my eyes but said nothing. *Little sisters*, I thought, annoyed.

After rolling up our sleeves and tying up our hair, Tara and I joined Theo, who was already at work in the back. By this point in our lives, we were like a well-oiled machine, both at work and at home. Each of us knew what project to begin and where to work.

I was so excited about crafting candles for the holidays, I had to get started. As I mixed, stirring clockwise, a poem—a chant—came to me.

Grant my wish

Grant my desire

I shall achieve all I aspire

I already have what I require

As I stirred the ingredients for the first batch of candles, the memory of the chant came to me. I closed my eyes and tried to remember. I was not sure where I was in this memory. I remember peeking through a crack, watching my mother and aunt chanting, their voices growing louder and louder, chanting in unison. They say that scent holds the strongest memory, although I'm not sure who 'they' are exactly.

Almost as soon as Theo unlocked the door, our first customer showed up. Mrs. Henrietta VanHoy bounced through the door as our tell-tale jingle announced her arrival. Mrs. VanHoy was a round, jolly, middle-aged woman, who always had a wide smile on her face. Each side of her smile was accented with deep dimples. Mrs. VanHoy was known in town by all, as she was married to Mr. Silas VanHoy, our mayor. You could describe Mrs. VanHoy as happy, alive, and even spirited. You could describe her husband as the inverse. Although Mr. VanHoy was round, he was full of sharp edges.

9

His angular nose protruded from a round face, anchored by thin lips, always deeply frowning. His personality was just as angular and sharp. He seemed to be in constant conflict with most of the locals. He made it clear on numerous occasions and to all who would listen, he was hoping to turn Seven Hills into a more 'commercial' tourist destination, filled with chain restaurants and stores.

"Good morning, Mrs. VanHoy!" Theodora said cheerfully, wiping her hands on her apron. "What can we do for you today?"

Mrs. VanHoy scanned the store before saying, "Why, hello girls! I have an order to pick up for some supplies for the Halloween parade and pageant."

"Oh, yes," Theodora said, checking the computer behind the counter before heading to the back room to, no doubt, grab boxes of packaged supplies.

"How is everything coming for the parade and pageant, Mrs. VanHoy?" I asked, while we waited, my eyes falling on her coffin nails, blood-red and shiny. The sight almost made me ill; I hate the sight of blood.

Mrs. VanHoy's large brown eyes shone brightly, "Just wonderful. I love this time of the year. The pumpkins. The decorations. All the festivities." She paused. "You know Sarah Tarleton, right?"

"Of course," I nodded.

Everyone knew Sarah Tarleton. Theodora, Tara, and I had grown up with her. She and I were in the same grade together. Even those who were not in the same grade as Sarah knew of Sarah. She was one of the most beautiful women in town, and almost every man over the age of 21 was chasing her around.

Sarah has always been beautiful, even as a child. She grew up to be even more beautiful. Sarah had won the All Hallows' Eve Pageant every year during the time in which she could enter; the duration of high school. I was always slightly jealous of Sarah. She was cool, energetic, and flawless. She was the opposite of me— without baggage, without secrets, and without insecurities. I was always floating, waiting for the next disaster.

Despite growing up in Seven Hills together, I had rarely interacted with Sarah. This was probably a good thing. Sarah was known, not only for her stunning looks, but also for her cruelty. As I recall, even when Sarah was a freshman, she could make senior girls cry. This was a rare feat in our small town, as freshman girls were expected to cow tail to the older girls. She would mercilessly pick on the other girls in high school. Luckily, I seemed to pass by, mostly unnoticed. Just once, I had a brief, drunken, interaction with her at a high school party. We were both at her boyfriend, Cliff Bishop's house. I do not remember the specifics, but Cliff, known for being a bit of womanizer, had apparently flirted with another girl at the party. Cliff had been the high school quarterback. Everyone swore he would play college ball, and after that, they would say time and again, he would 'go pro.' Cliff never made it out of town, not even to college. He ended up as a part-time insurance salesman and did various other odd jobs in Seven Hills.

Deidra had dragged me to the party that night in a skirt so short that I tugged at it all night long. I remember standing in the bathroom upstairs, just checking my makeup in the mirror, when Sarah burst through the door and dashed straight to the toilet. Heaving, she unloaded the night's drinks into the bowl. Before I knew it, I was holding her hair, putting a cold washcloth on her neck. *Why were women always punishing themselves for the bad behavior of men?* I was surprised Sarah would do this. She seemed to be the type to punish others. After a few minutes of heaving and purging, she seemed to regain her senses. She turned around and looked at me, with her mouth caked with vomit residue, and her mascara running. This seemed to be the first time she saw me; the first time she even knew I was there. *Who did she think was helping her?* I had wondered. Perhaps, beautiful girls imagined angels held their hair and put cool washcloths on their necks if they were ever sick.

"Treasure," she said, almost like a question. For a moment, I thought maybe she did not know who I was.

"Yeah," I responded, as if to confirm I was, in fact, Treasure.

"You're strange, aren't you?"

Deidra and I left the party.

"Ok, I found the order," Theodora bellowed, interrupting my thoughts as she came out of the back room. She plopped a large box down near the register and started pulling out each carefully, hand-crafted item, one by one. Mrs. VanHoy had ordered a large amount of makeup, primer, face paint, and face and body lotion. It looked like she had ordered some homemade perfumes as well.

"The perfumes are for me," she said with a giggle, her dimples on full display. I wondered if she ever used the perfumes she purchased. Every time I saw Mrs. VanHoy, she smelled amazing, but never like any of our concoctions. I remembered once a friendly, female tourist had inquired about her perfume. She relayed a name that I couldn't recall now if my life depended on it, but I had googled it then. It was extremely expensive, European, and it was her signature scent. You could smell it on her wherever she went. Often, it lingered long after she was gone. I wondered how much of the expensive bottle she used each day and how the VanHoys could possibly afford such luxuries.

Mrs. VanHoy giggled, her body and expensive gold earrings shaking in unison. "We all deserve a treat every now and then. I just adore the scents you all come up with! Well, anyway, as I was saying…Sarah, she is such a dear! She has been helping me with everything for the parade and pageant. It seems as if we are on track to get everything done and ready on time, but I'm still counting on you girls to make the decorations for the Seven Hills float. Dr. Jackman will be giving the presentation about the women on the float, of course. Hopefully, all will go well with the sound system. What a disaster last year was!"

For the last several years, Dr. Ronnie Jackman rode on the Seven Hills Historical Society float, mostly without disaster. Last year, however, Dr. Jackman's microphone refused to cooperate. He seemed to be trying to yell his lecture as his microphone faded in and out, before giving up and just waving to the crowd. Dr. Ronnie Jackman was Seven Hills' local historian. His area of expertise was historical Paganism and Witchcraft, although his work extended beyond that and into modern-day 'witch hunts' like the Satanic Panic of the 1980s. His work seemed to center around what were perceived to be 'deviant' belief systems and practices and how fears surrounding these beliefs could turn deadly. Other than the five women that suffered during the 1600s, he was Seven Hills' only 'celebrity.' He was a frequent guest on *PBS* and *The History Channel*. He even wrote several books. If I remembered correctly, one book even hit *The New York Times* best-seller list. I never read any of his books on Seven Hills. Growing up here, I felt I didn't need to. We were surrounded by the history every day.

Like Sarah, Ronnie graduated with me. Growing up, he was a small, shy, brown-haired boy that kept to himself. But, as the saying goes, he was 'as smart as a whip.' He seemed to win every spelling bee and math tournament. He was our Valedictorian. Granted, with a graduating class of 80 students, that was not too difficult. However, there was no doubt that Ronnie was brilliant. His research was well received by critics and academic peers alike. Upon graduation, he moved away for college and didn't visit much. He returned home for good a year or so ago, declaring that Seven Hills was the best place for him to study and to be immersed in history. I had once read in an interview that he believed that Seven Hills was 'his muse.'

"Of course! I am always here to help," Theodora said enthusiastically, breaking into my thoughts about Ronnie. "You know I love a good craft."

Tara and I snorted, and Theodora whipped her head up from the register. She gave us a slight look of annoyance, one of her eyebrows arching up above the other.

"You need to start loving to date," Tara said loud enough for Mrs. VanHoy to hear, who was partially focused on applying red lipstick using a hand compact. "Your eggs are getting all shriveled up," Tara added.

Mrs. VanHoy looked horrified for second. She looked at Theodora and said, "Oh my! Do not let her pick on you! Theodora, you are one of the best women in town!"

Mrs. VanHoy added, "Why, I do not know what I would do without Theodora always helping me out! There is so much to do with everything going on!"

We all turned to the window as we suddenly heard shouting in the street. Deidra could be seen arguing with a man outside of Seven Sweets. The angry faces and shouting were in direct contrast to the sweet looking bakery with its bright pastel pink and teal awning. Mrs. VanHoy, Theodora, Tara, and I moved in unison to the window, trying to avoid the fresh herbs hanging to dry as we looked out.

"Oh, my word!" Mrs. VanHoy gasped, moving a rope of dried rosemary out of her face. Her whole body seemed to be pulsing with anger, suddenly turning electric.

"Is that Mr. VanHoy?" Tara asked with a shocked expression across her face, turning to Mrs. VanHoy, as if demanding some sort of answer.

Before we knew it, Mrs. VanHoy was out the door and across the street with the three of us trailing not far behind. I could hear the sleigh bells crashing into the glass door as we ran. Mrs. VanHoy was surprisingly fast, despite wearing extremely high black pumps. Red bottoms, of course.

"How dare you try to intimidate me!" Deidra bellowed, shaking violently. Her face was full of pent-up anger. "You are *not* going to bully me into selling my shop!"

Mr. VanHoy's large face was bright red with anger. Mrs. VanHoy put her perfectly manicured hand on her husband's arm, which he brushed off forcefully. I wondered what their home life was like, especially when he was angered.

"Dear, let's go," she said nervously, pulling her tweed jacket around her tightly. "That is enough for one day."

He glanced at his wife briefly before turning back to Deidra declaring aggressively, "*I* know what's best for this town and community. Deidra, *you* need to grow up and do what is best for everyone. Nobody cares about your little shop."

Theodora, Tara, and I all had our mouths open in disbelief. Tara started to protest. She was small, but always seemed ready for a fight or a challenge. "You don't know what you're talking about VanHoy. Why don't you just get out of here and leave everyone alone!"

VanHoy ignored Tara. He always ignored the Culpepper girls, never made eye contact, and never entered the shop. Suddenly, I wondered why that was. *Why did he avoid us?* Sarah Tarleton's words rang in my head, *you're strange, aren't you?*

Deidra bellowed again, shaking, "do you think a Value Mart is really what is best for this community? We are tourist location! Part of what sets us apart is the small-town, tight-knit feel of this community! Do you think Value Mart is a part of that, especially so close to the downtown area? Small businesses will go under. This is a horrible plan for our community!" she raged, practically stamping her feet, like a child.

"Deidra, you know nothing about what is best for our community. You are a little girl with a little bakery," he said venomously. "In the big picture, you do not matter!"

"Silas!" Mrs. VanHoy exclaimed loudly. "That is quite enough! Time for us to go!" Her whole body was vibrating, her shiny black Chanel purse almost falling from her arms. She looked like she wanted to wring his neck.

Mr. VanHoy looked at Deidra closely and then around the street. Several business owners and patrons had now come out of their shops to see what all the commotion was about. There were no less than 15 people standing in the street now, observing the spectacle. VanHoy seemed to visibly calm down after noticing the attention he was attracting. He smoothed down his tie and his pin-striped jacket, and then ran a hand over his slick black hair.

"Deidra," he said with more measure, "we are not finished with this discussion. I regret raising my voice, but I do not regret the sentiments. Seven Hills must progress. Value Mart would be an excellent way to bring in more jobs and income to our community. Perhaps, you do not need to close your little business but to move it. Just think about it. Try to do what is best for all the Seven Hills' residents."

Deidra rolled her eyes in response and crossed her arms, indicating she was done with the topic of conversation. "You need to leave," she said steadily.

"You need to leave," VanHoy retorted.

"You need to leave," Deidra stated again, quieter this time, dropping her arms, her tiny hands formed into fists.

"Come on Silas," Mrs. VanHoy said, taking his arm in hers. This time, he did not shrug her off. Then she turned to Theodora, "Theo, maybe I can pick up my box tomorrow?" Theodora nodded without saying a word. Neither VanHoy made eye contact with any of the women or the spectators, as they got into their sleek, shiny-black Cadillac and drove away.

All of us stood silently, stunned by what had just transpired. Eventually, as if in slow motion, the people who observed the scene went back into their respective businesses or back to their shopping. Theodora hurried back to The Alchemist to lock it up before we all convened in Seven Sweets. We collapsed into the bright teal chairs around a small circular table near the front of the shop. Seven

Sweets was a small, quaint bakery, with a seating area about the size of a classroom. There was a full, private kitchen in the back, but it did not offer much space for sitting, as each inch was used for some sort of purpose. Deidra grabbed a pot of coffee and poured us all hot mugfuls, as we began to calm down. Any customers that were sipping coffee and eating treats when the commotion began seemed to have left wordlessly. Now the shop was empty, except for a few tourists, no doubt gossiping about the morning's spectacle.

Finally, Deidra spoke. Her voice was measured, but her green eyes were still blazing with fury. "I watched him drop off Mrs. VanHoy at The Alchemist and park. I knew when I saw him approaching the shop that all hell was about to break loose. He never comes in here unless he is 'encouraging' me to sell or move. He thinks we should allow room to put a Value Mart here. Apparently, Seven Sweets is located on the edge of where the parking lot would be."

As she finished, the exasperation Deidra felt could be seen clearly on her face.

"That is ridiculous!" I exclaimed. I realized customers were still there and lowered my voice. "A Value Mart right smack down in the middle of downtown would ruin the feel of our town!"

"Not to mention the impact corporations can have on local businesses," Theodora added, looking a bit worried.

"Value Marts are eyesores!" Tara exclaimed. "I would rather they put a strip club next to Seven

Sweets!" We all laughed at Tara's comment, breaking the tension.

"This is the third time he has been here talking about his stupid Value Mart. I feel like he is threatening me," Deidra said, a frown on her pretty face. Her perfectly manicured eyebrows knitted together in a worried expression.

"He can't do that!" Theodora said, her voice rising. Her head was shaking, and black wisps of hair began to fall away from her ponytail. In this moment, she reminded me so much of Mom. "He can't come in and intimidate people to sell their businesses! It is absolutely harassment."

"We should check in with Paul and Mike, to see how they're doing," I added.

Paul Richards owned The Craft, housed in a tall, red-sided building next to Seven Sweets. It is a delightful local shop where you can go to create flower arrangements or pottery, and purchase items for scrapbooking. Like in the old-West photo shops found in theme parks, Paul even set up a station where you could dress up like Halloween monsters to take pictures with your family and friends. The Craft was beloved by townspeople and tourists alike. It would be unlikely that Paul would ever sell, especially because he lived in a small apartment above the store.

Next door to The Craft, was Mike Howard's small hardware store, The Witch's Hammer. It had an old-time feel; walking into The Witch's Hammer felt like you were entering a hardware store from the 1950s. The Witch's Hammer had blue siding, blue and white awnings, and large planters full of flowers in front.

In large letters, The Witch's Hammer arched above the shop entrance. The clever name came from the insidious book, *Malleus Maleficarum*, written by Heinrich Kramer and Jacob Springer. Published in the 1400s, *Malleus Maleficarum* was 'literature' meant to 'educate' the public on witches, with a focus on how to find and punish them. Many people throughout the ages suffered because of the misinformation in that book. A small shiver went up my spine just thinking about it. I pulled my wool sweater down over my hands, and I took a sip of hot coffee to warm me up.

"It is obvious that he doesn't take your business seriously, Deidra. He kept calling it 'your little business'. He's gross," Tara declared, a look of disgust on her face. "I feel like we should toilet paper his mansion!"

We all laughed again.

"I feel bad for Mrs. VanHoy. She is so nice," I said empathically.

"She enables him," Tara responded rolling her eyes. Tara was notorious for having minimal compassion towards others, especially those who hurt the people that she loved. Deidra was like a third big sister to her.

I nodded slightly, "well, *she* has to live with him."

"If I had to live with him," Deidra said flatly, lowering her voice, "He would be dead already."

Chapter 2

Theodora locked the back door of The Alchemist as Tara and I walked to our separate vehicles. We decided to leave just a little earlier than normal to continue working on the decorations for the All Hallows' Eve Pageant. Theodora opened the rear door of her Chevrolet Caprice Classic station wagon, light blue with faux wood paneling, and loaded our crafting supplies. I could not help but smile. Theodora loved that car. It had been our mother's, and although it would be far more economical to get a newer vehicle, Theodora especially liked keeping it around. Throughout the years, Theodora had the seats reupholstered, the body repaired from minor fender benders and rust, and the engine replaced twice. But she would never sell or scrap it.

"It's practical for the business," Theodora always said whenever a mechanic advised against continued repairs. Theodora kept a sachet of our mom's favorite herbs under the front seat, so it continued to smell like her–lavender and sage–that became particularly fragrant on warm days. Tara and I knew it was not about being practical or even frugal. The car was Theodora's connection to Mom, and we would never question any repair or expense.

Within minutes, we reached the edge of town and began a ten-minute journey on State Route 2 towards our family home. The winding, two-lane road was surrounded by a thick paneling of old trees in full fall colors, broken every now and again by a driveway. As the trees became less dense and the view opened up, I started to see the edge of our rolling property, which had been owned by our family for over 200 years. The outer acres were outlined by weathered, split rail fencing that we meticulously repaired every spring. Closer to the house, a two-foot-tall stone wall replaced the wood fencing in the front of the property, running perfectly parallel with the old state route.

After a slight curve, the 18th century stone house, known in Seven Hills as Culpepper Manor, came into view. Theodora, who was leading our caravan, slowed to pull into the gravel driveway. Built in 1799, the house rested several hundred feet from the roadway. We slowly made our way through the dips and curves of the driveway we all knew by heart. Much like my sister's station wagon, the house had received its share of updates and repairs throughout the years. Earlier generations added modern plumbing and electricity. When outbuildings burned down or fell, they were replaced by newer structures with the latest technology. At one time, the estate encompassed nearly 1,000 acres. Over time, plots were sold to cover lean years. Now, other family homes could be seen creeping over the horizon.

Our mother rebuilt a barn when Theodora was small, and, at around 30 years old, it was the newest structure on the property. My sisters and I knocked down part of the east wall of the barn ten years ago, and added an attached greenhouse, so we could grow certain herbs year-round. While the barn was still structurally sound, it really needed paint, but we all liked the weathered look. The house and property were expensive to maintain; but, between the three of us, we managed.

We pulled up to the front of the house and turned off the vehicles. To the casual observer, the gardens that nearly overtook the front of the house may have seemed haphazard or overgrown. But, in reality, the plantings were all meticulously planned. Certain herbs needed more access to sunlight than others. Some plants provided nutrients to the soil that other plants needed. Everything had its place. I stepped out of my car and walked over to the west garden, as Theodora and Tara unloaded the station wagon. I loved walking through the gardens as the sun started to settle, seeming to melt into the earth. The orange glow softly illuminated the stone pathways. The air was slightly cool and still. I took in a deep breath and slowly exhaled. Generations of Culpepper women had walked these stone paths, each showing the next where to plant and how to get the most out of their crops. These gardens connected us to our mother, grandmother, and our eternal mother, the earth.

We did not use chemical fertilizers or insect repellants. We had a couple of natural tricks up our sleeve if a particular insect or animal was causing a problem, but generally, we let it go. Our gardens were as much for the land as they were for our business. We worked with Mother Nature, and she provided us with the most bountiful harvests. As the sun fell further, I clipped a few flowers and gathered two ripened squashes and headed for the front door.

The oversized, heavy wooden door at the front of the manor house was original to the home. Its deeply carved, dark mahogany had stood the test of the time. Only the hardware had been restored. I pulled open the door and stepped inside.

Upon entering Culpepper Manor, guests are immediately greeted by a spacious foyer with a ceiling to the second floor and a large, central staircase in front of them. The walls are covered with antique wood paneling that makes the whole house feel warm and safe. To the left, the east wing of the manor includes the kitchen, laundry room, and dining room, with guest bedrooms and former staff quarters directly above. The west wing includes the living room, library, solarium, drawing room, and office. Our bedrooms are on the second floor of the west wing.

I put my coat in the foyer closet and took a moment to marvel at the grandeur of the foyer and the delicious smells wafting from the kitchen. All who entered the house remarked on its enchanting warmth and air of calmness. I could remember, although vaguely, when we were much younger our mother and Aunt Elaina hosted family and friends, just as their mother had before them. Laughter and love had filled these halls for generations. We firmly believed those emotions lingered in the woodwork. Some visitors mentioned feeling a little spooked from time to time–perhaps catching a glance of a shadowy figure moving across a doorway–or feeling a cool breeze in an otherwise temperate room. There were no vengeful spirits at Culpepper Manor. Both my mother and Aunt Elaina, who lived with us throughout our childhood, casually remarked, it was a family member just popping in to see what was happening in the house.

I made my way down the hallway to the kitchen.

"Treasure!" Tara called as soon as I entered the doorway. She had a flower in her hand like a pointer. "Tell Theodora that I absolutely would have won the beauty pageant when I was a senior. I *chose* not to participate so I wouldn't ruin the lives of all those other girls."

Theodora, at the stove in her trusty apron, snorted.

"Our mother is the only one in this family who has ever been teen royalty," I said back to Tara. "I don't think 'old hag witch' was what the judges were looking for when you were in high school," I said laughing.

"Yeah, you weren't exactly reflecting 'high school beauty queen' with that look," Theodora said chiming in.

"Whatever!" Tara huffed.

"I am sure you would have won had you actually participated," Theodora said in her motherly voice.

I rolled my eyes and walked over to the stove. "What smells so good?"

"Chicken pot pie," Theodora said, stirring the stew pot. "Just a couple of more minutes to finish here, then I'll pop these in the oven," she said, gesturing to the mini pie shells on the center island that she had previously prepared.

The annual Seven Hills All Hallows' Eve Pageant was not a traditional beauty pageant; definitely not the way pageants were portrayed on television. I once watched a television program on a lazy afternoon in which pageant parents had spray-painted their children's skin with bright orange bronzer. Many on the show adorned their children with eyelashes that could have doubled as push-brooms. Most teens that entered the Seven Hills All Hallows' Eve Pageant wore simple outfits and modest makeup. Unlike the television show, the pageant was much more of a town celebration than a competition. It was open to all high school girls, and girls could enter, and win, in multiple years. Participating in the pageant was considered a rite of passage in Seven Hills, and most girls had entered at least once. Our mother, who by all accounts had been the town darling growing up, had entered her senior year and was crowned queen. Aunt Elaina had also participated in the pageant, and they both fondly, and frequently, spoke about their experiences. As adults, they volunteered every year to make decorations and products for the contestants.

During the first round, participants wore formal wear provided at no cost through sponsorships from local businesses. Since the pageant began in the 1930s, the Culpepper family, and later The Alchemist, had sponsored several girls for the pageant, including our mother. Other rounds consisted of questions to the girls. In the final round, participants wore costumes; and honestly, that was the best part of the pageant. Participants and sponsors alike did their best to come up with something new and creative every year. Some of the costumes were scary, but generally, most costumes were bright and cheery, reflecting the very nature of Seven Hills itself. After the final round, the judges would select one girl to be queen and four others to serve on the court. The honorees would then ride in the annual parade through town the following year.

Our mother and Aunt Elaina had encouraged my sisters and me to participate but without much luck. Growing up, we did not feel the same way about Seven Hills as our mother, and the pageant always seemed like something the 'other girls' did. With all my mother's brilliance, she did not seem to notice that everything in Seven Hills had shifted for her daughters. Perhaps she did, but she was trying to keep things as 'normal' as possible. Perhaps, my sisters and I did not enter because we all resented my mom a bit for making us strange by association. Theo and I quietly avoided the pageant, opting to make decorations behind the scenes. Tara was a bit more vocal in her distaste for Seven Hills and the pageant itself. It was during her senior year that she opted to show up to the event dressed like an old hag witch. She sat in the back in protest, which caused quite a stir.

Not long after Tara's hag-witch stunt, our mother passed away. There was no warning that something had been wrong. She was seemingly fine one minute, gone the next. Cancer quickly taking her.

Her death rattled our world. Tara, already struggling to live in Seven Hills, decided to leave.

Tara wanted us to sell The Alchemist, but Aunt Elaina encouraged us to keep the business. Theo and I decided to stay, and that first fall after our mother's passing had been especially hard. I remember that Beth Stoker, a classmate of my mother's, wandered into the store not too long after her passing.

"How are you girls holding up?" she asked, patting us with brightly manicured hands. Her arms keeping her expensive bag close to her, as if we might snatch it at any minute.

"We are holding up," Theo said with a sad, but resilient smile.

"So young," Beth said to no one in particular. She shook her head hard, theatrically, insincerely.

"Yes," was all I could manage to say.

"The guilt," she said quietly, before she was asked to leave. She never returned.

Life, like nature, moved on. Winter gave way to spring and then summer. Soon, October arrived again. Theo and I had given up on the festivities in Seven Hills, until one day, I came home after work to find Theo in the kitchen working on pageant decorations. At first, I did not know what to think about it. After a couple of days of watching her happily toiling away, I found myself wandering into the kitchen to help. We would talk about childhood memories and laugh, and through that process started to understand why Mom and Aunt Elaina loved preparing for the pageant so much. Ever since, we have continued to volunteer and make decorations as a way to feel closer to our family. Many seasons passed before Tara returned to Culpepper Manor. The first pageant season after her return, without comment or complaint, she walked into the kitchen and started helping with the decorations. The three of us had been doing it together ever since. Slowly, things returned to a normal, happy place.

Mom and Aunt Elaina updated the family kitchen about ten years ago. Although the space was quite practical, the cabinetry and appliances were all well past their prime. As we spent more time together in the kitchen than any other room in the house, we needed an updated workspace. In addition to basic meal preparation, we used the kitchen for The Alchemist, necessitating the need for larger appliances and more counter space.

During the remodel, they purchased a commercial-grade gas stove. While ten burners and two large capacity ovens were way too much for a basic family meal, it made perfect sense for the multiple times of year we produced large quantities of salves, lotions, and soaps. A process that took a week before could now be accomplished in one Saturday.

To the right of the stove, spanning the length of the kitchen, were new oak cabinets with a darker-harvest stain, earthy green and brown marble countertops, and a large farm sink with a pull-down sprayer. The center island was 12 feet long, with the same marble countertop, but with open shelving, filled with various pots and pans. We kept a couple of stools around the island, which was our favorite place for quick work-week meals.

On the other side of the island were large pantry cabinets, a commercial-size refrigerator, a separate, commercial-size freezer, and the former staff staircase to the second floor. The former cabinets on this wall had been original built-ins with hundreds of layers of paint. In the summer months, you could hardly open some of the cabinets, and they weren't very deep, making them quite impractical. The decision to remove the cabinets was a difficult one, since they had been in the home since its original construction, but Mom and Aunt Elaina ultimately replaced them with modern cabinets with slide shelving. I removed the doors and stripped the paint off of the original built-ins, revealing the beautiful hardwood hidden underneath. After refinishing the wood, I had them moved upstairs to the sitting area of my bedroom, where I use them for bookcases.

I joined Tara at the ten-foot kitchen table that often doubled as a workspace. Scattered about were piles of dried flowers, ribbons, and mini pumpkins. A pile of dried cornstalks sat to the left of the kitchen fireplace, which Tara had stocked with extra logs. The heat from this fire adequately warmed the kitchen, allowing us to reserve gas heating for the bedrooms and living areas. To the right of the fireplace were large wooden racks, loaded with drying flower and herb bunches. During the summer, we had a large area in the barn reserved for drying, but we often used the kitchen during the cold and rainy seasons.

"What are we thinking?" I asked, surveying what had already been completed. "A couple of free-standing cornstalk bunches for the pageant stage? More entry swags?"

"I think that sounds good," Tara said, putting some finishing touches on a table centerpiece. "And

I think we should do paper lanterns for the front of the pageant stage. Those looked great last year."

"I agree," Theodora added from the stove. "We received a lot of compliments about those." Theodora popped the pies into the oven and joined us at the table. "So, what was the deal with Deidra and VanHoy today? Now he's confronting people in the street?"

"I don't know," I said, gathering a pen knife and stencil to start constructing the lanterns. "Poor Deidra. She already told him no. Her business is successful, and she's especially busy this time of year. Tourists don't want to come here and visit Value Mart. They can do that at home. They want the local shops."

"Exactly," Theodora said, while constructing a large bow. "This time of year is great for all of us. We generate enough business in the fall to keep the store opened all year. If it weren't for that, we would have a terrible time keeping this house."

"Mike said VanHoy had been in The Witch's Hammer twice to try to talk to him," I recounted, shaking my head. "Mike said he managed to avoid him each time. I can only imagine that is going to get harder and harder to do."

"Paul said VanHoy cornered him in the produce section of the grocery store—at the tomato bin," Theodora added. "Paul especially has a lot to lose. Even if he decided to move the business, there is no way he could compete with Value Mart's pricing."

"Well, VanHoy better not come into The Alchemist and try to talk to us," Tara steamed. "That'd be the last time he would have use of his eyes. *I'll pluck his little eyeballs out!*" She said in a witchy voice.

"Tara, there is no way that man is coming into The Alchemist," I said laughing. "I think he's scared of you...scared of *us!*"

"Good!" Tara bellowed boisterously. "He should be!"

Tara was such a ball of contradictions. She railed against the family business when she was younger, furious that we had been pigeonholed into a trade. After she left home, we rarely heard from her. She had stopped back every now and again, usually for a holiday, and then would be on her way. She lived all over the country, and even did a couple of months floating around Europe. Theodora and I were both shocked when she showed up on the manor doorsteps and announced that she was coming back to stay. I still do not think she particularly likes the store, but she vocalizes her complaints less and less often. The moment anyone outside of the family threatens the business, however, she transforms into its greatest defender, primed to attack whomever she perceives to be a threat.

"Really, I do believe VanHoy is scared of all of us," Theodora said laughing. "The three sisters living alone in this big stone house.... No one really knows what we're doing over here...."

"We're all standing over the cauldron, cooking up a spell so he'll lose his fortune...and his manhood!" Tara said, again using a flower as a pointer for dramatic effect.

"Someone should tell him we have a gas stove," I said. We all laughed.

The evening slowly slipped by as my sisters and I continued to work on decorations. When the pot pies were ready, we took a break and gathered around the kitchen island. I cut into the crust of one of those savory concoctions, allowing the steam to escape. After a minute, I took a slow bite, allowing the thick sauce, tender chicken, perfectly softened vegetables, and flaky crust to dance on my palette. This was comfort food at its finest! As we enjoyed, we passed around a bottle of red wine and started telling stories of Halloweens past.

"The absolute worst costume I remember seeing downtown was Donald Henson's zombie, slash, mummy, slash, nose-picking, I don't even know what," Theodora said, wrinkling her nose. "Remember he made that fake snot out of oatmeal and was eating it? Ick!" She said, making a face while holding her throat. "I seriously have not been able to eat oatmeal again without starting to think about it. And then, when I think about it, I can't finish eating the oatmeal!"

After the parade and pageant were over, residents and tourists alike gathered in the large gazebo in the town square for a party. Businesses set up booths to promote their business or sell a few of their wares, and there was usually a stand or two selling treats like caramel apples or funnel cakes. Tables were assembled inside the gazebo, leaving just enough room for a dance floor. A DJ was hired, and there was always a bar stocked with alcohol. All Hallows' Eve was a night for celebration. And a celebration it was. The soiree had no start time and, perhaps most importantly, no end time. No end time allowed for some crazy stories the next day and created fodder for town gossip for weeks thereafter.

"That costume was amazing!" Tara countered. "Definitely a top ten. Anything that makes other people want to vomit gets extra points. However, best costume of all time?" Tara continued, "Brett Halpert as the Kool-Aid man!"

"Oh, no!" Theodora and I said in unison.

"Oh, yeah!" Tara said, clutching her wine glass to her chest. "It was amazing. I could have married him that night."

Brett Halpert was in his thirties at the time of the Kool-Aid incident and had a rather sizeable waist. Instead of wearing an actual costume, he painted himself in red body paint using what must have been black shoe polish on his chest for the Kool-Aid man's eyes and mouth. It had been a little too much of Brett Halpert, in my opinion, but Tara had a weird appreciation for big, hairy, and sweaty.

"I nearly died when he walked into the store a week later and asked for something to help remove the black paint." Theodora said, shaking her head.

"The man needed help!" I giggled.

"But I didn't need to see it!" Theodora shrieked.

It had been pretty funny, though. Brett came by the store and told us he couldn't get the paint off. While Theodora was asking him questions about his skin and the ingredients of the paint, Brett took his shirt off so Theodora could see for herself. Theodora had turned bright red, absolutely mortified. I couldn't stop laughing and had to run to the back of the store.

"I wish I could have seen it…. Mmmmm." Tara said, closing her eyes.

I laughed while Theodora looked disgusted.

"What about you, Treasure?" Theodora asked. "Favorite downtown costume?"

The truth was, I absolutely loved them all. The scary, the homemade, the beautiful, and the creative. But of course, there were always those hidden gems that stood out slightly higher than the rest.

"Ronnie Jackman as Daniel Defoe."

"What?!" Tara demanded. "His costumes are the worst! He always looks the same and boring. Who is Daniel Defoe anyway?"

"The author—you know, *Robinson Crusoe*?" I retorted.

"Yeah, don't care," Tara yawned. "Ronnie needs to get a life."

After he moved back to Seven Hills, Ronnie and I would run into each other every now and again, mostly at the library.

"I thought it was smart," I explained. "Most people don't put that kind of thought into their costumes."

"Yeah, because most people aren't that boring," Tara countered. "He's weird."

"We're all weird," Theodora interjected.

"Speak for yourself!" Tara snapped. "I'm going as a sexy kitten this year. The costume really enhances the 'girls,'" Tara continued, clutching the underside of her chest.

"Shocker!" I said, putting my head to the side. "Tara going as a sexy-something. I never would have guessed!"

"Jealous," Tara stated, as she stood to put her dishes in the sink. "I gotta catch me a new man."

"I wonder who the sexy kitten costume will catch?" I said, stroking my chin.

"Most likely someone rich," Tara said confidently.

Theodora and I laughed, as this was a long shot. We cleared the rest of the dishes from the island, then resumed our crafting at the large table. As the clock neared twelve, we decided to call it a night. We took a moment to review what we had created and were happy with the results. A few finishing touches here and there, but nothing we couldn't handle quickly the next day.

"Goodnight," Tara hollered, as she headed towards the staff staircase in the kitchen.

"Remember, we are all working together in the morning," Theodora hollered back. "I will leave without you if you are not ready on time!"

"Yeah, yeah, got it...," we heard Tara mumble as she disappeared up the stairs. Theodora rolled her eyes, and I laughed. Theodora slipped up the back staircase, and I followed behind a few moments later.

Using the staff staircase in the kitchen meant that, to reach our bedrooms on the west side of the house, we had to walk past the guest and former staff quarters on the second floor. The house was especially dark, with the only light coming from dimmed sconces that lined the expansive hallway. Crossing over the landing area of the large central staircase, my bedroom was the first door on the left.

The family bedrooms in Culpepper Manor were much more than typical bedrooms in a regular, single-family home. Each bedroom was like a little suite, as each encompassed three separate rooms. The hallway doors entered into a sitting area. French doors in the sitting area led to the sleeping room, and each sleeping room contained a bed, walk-in closet, and en suite bathroom. Each of our bedrooms was uniquely decorated, reflecting our individual style and preferences.

Immediately to the right of the hallway door, my sitting room contained the refinished built-ins from the kitchen, all loaded with books, pictures, movies, candles, and little trinket souvenirs I've collected over time. An over-stuffed loveseat and chair sat in the center of the room, facing the wood fireplace on the west wall. The rear wall was covered with over-size windows looking over the tranquil, rolling wooded landscape. I had curtains on these windows, but I never closed them. None of the properties behind the manor house were close enough to even see, and I enjoyed stepping out in the morning, or sometimes in the middle of the night, to watch the tree branches flowing in the breeze.

On the east wall were French doors leading to my sleeping area. I opened the left door and stepped inside. Typically, I liked starting a fire in the sitting room and then curling up on the couch with a good book in the evenings, but it was far too late tonight, especially when I had to be at work early the next morning. Instead, I stripped off my clothes and pulled on an extra-large t-shirt and velvet lounge pants that were perfect for sleeping on a cool, autumn evening. As I settled into my bed, I couldn't help but think of Deidra and her confrontation with VanHoy earlier in the day. *What a mess*, I thought to myself. My mind wandered over that for several minutes, but then exhaustion got the better of me. Just as I started to drift off to sleep, I caught the distinct scents of lavender and sage.

I was awoken suddenly by my phone chirping on the bedside table. It was Theodora.

"Crap!" I exclaimed, jumping out of bed. I opened the text.

"Are you awake?" she asked.

"Yes!!" I answered back. I hurriedly popped into the shower and threw on some clothes. Just as I was exiting my room, Tara joined me in the hallway.

"These mornings are the worst," she groaned, putting on some sunglasses.

"It's still dark outside," I said curiously.

"Don't care," she said, joining me down the central staircase. "It's that kind of morning."

"Good morning, sisters!" Theodora said, cheerfully at the front door. Tara and I both groaned in response. She was entirely too enthusiastic in the mornings. She never went out at night and was probably in bed most evenings by 9 pm, but Theodora loved those early mornings. She had probably been up for hours. "I've already packed the car," she said, pulling open the front door.

"Great," I said half-heartedly.

All I needed was some coffee and a breakfast pastry from Deidra, and I would be good to go. Just thinking about Deidra's coffee started to perk me up. I could already taste it. We exited the manor house and paused.

"Wait, who's driving?" Tara asked.

We looked around at each other, waiting for someone to speak.

"Well, I'm going to be dropping off some products for the pageant at some point this morning," I explained.

"I'm supposed to pick up some sheep's wool from our supplier around 1 pm. That's at least a 40-minute trip," Tara added.

"Are we seriously going to be driving separately to the store again?" Theodora asked.

"Looks like it," I said, heading towards my vehicle.

"Which means, we all didn't have to be up this early," Tara said annoyed.

"We all need to be at the store!" Theodora countered. "So, I guess I'll see you there!" she said, climbing into the station wagon.

We entered our vehicles and started down the driveway to begin our journey back to town. I looked in my rearview mirror to see Tara still wearing her sunglasses. *How in the world can she see to drive like that?*

As we neared the store, I immediately saw a police cruiser and dark-blue sedan outside of Seven

Sweets. We all quickly parked and jumped out of our vehicles, exchanging worried looks.

"What's going on?" Theodora asked.

"I have no idea," I stammered.

Just as we were getting ready to cross the street, the front door of Seven Sweets opened and a police officer exited, holding the door for Deidra and a man in a suit. Deidra obviously looked upset.

"Deidra!" I yelled, hurriedly crossing the street. "Deidra! What's going on?"

"VanHoy is dead!" Deidra shrieked. "They think I killed him!"

Theodora, Tara, and I stopped in our tracks, right in the middle of the street.

"Wh-what?" I asked when I found my breath.

"He's dead!" she hollered, choking on tears. "I didn't do anything!" she continued.

"Ma'am," the man in the suit said sternly, "again, we are not suggesting that you did. We merely want to question you about the altercation you had with Mr. VanHoy yesterday afternoon."

"Altercation?!" Tara said, charging towards the man in the suit. "It was an argument, first of all; and Deidra didn't start it. She was being harassed by VanHoy!"

The police officer, who we could now see was Travis Hodge, someone we have known since grade school, stepped in front of Tara, just as she reached the man in the suit.

"Woah, Miss Culpepper," Travis said. "You need to calm down!"

"'Miss Culpepper' what?!" Tara screamed. "Get out of my way, Travis!"

"Tara!" Theodora and I both yelled grabbing her from behind.

"Come on, Tara," Travis pleaded. "There is no need for this; just calm down!"

"Don't tell me to calm down!" Tara continued to yell. "Where are you taking Deidra?"

"Just tell us what's going on Travis," I said, tightening my grip on Tara.

"They're taking me to the police station!" Deidra shrieked. "The police station! What is happening?"

Deidra dropped her head into her hands and started sobbing. Deidra's sobbing only intensified the situation, and we all three began hurling questions at Travis and the man in the suit. The man in the suit opened the front door of the sedan and had Deidra sit. He shut the door, turned towards us, placed his pinkies in his mouth, and loudly whistled. Theodora, Tara, and I stopped shouting, clearly startled.

"Good morning, ladies. I'm Detective Mike Harrison, Sheriff's Office. I am handling the VanHoy investigation. Now, everyone needs to take a breath."

"Sir," Theodora stated through a tense jaw. "We could all be much calmer if someone would explain to us what's happening."

"Mr. VanHoy was found murdered last night." Detective Harrison explained. "We understand Ms. Parker had an altercation with Mr. VanHoy yesterday afternoon—"

Just as Tara was about to interrupt, Detective Harrison raised his hand to cut her off. "'Altercation' means a noisy, heated argument, Miss...uh...Culpepper, wasn't it? It's our understanding that the argument was noisy and heated, taking place right in this street, with numerous witnesses. Isn't that correct?"

"Yes," Tara responded flatly.

"We are here this morning just to question Ms. Parker about the incident. She is not a suspect. She is not under arrest. She is upset, and this," he said, pointing to the three of us, "isn't helping. Once she is able to talk to us, she's free to leave. You'll notice she's not in handcuffs nor is she sitting in the back seat, the place where suspects and people under arrest sit."

I rolled my eyes. What a complete jerk.

"Forgive us," Theodora said sarcastically. "It's not every day our best friend is questioned in a murder investigation."

"She needs a lawyer," Tara spat. "She shouldn't be going anywhere with you without a lawyer."

"Tara, she's just coming in for questioning as a witness," Travis explained. "She doesn't need a lawyer."

"I don't believe anything you say, Travis! Of course, some cop would say someone doesn't need a lawyer," Tara countered. "I watch *Law & Order*! You always need a lawyer!"

"Again," clearly annoyed, Detective Harrison began massaging the bridge of his nose with his thumb and pointer finger, "Ms. Parker is not under arrest for murder. She doesn't even have to answer our questions. She agreed to help, and we're taking her to the station to show her some pictures and to allow her to calm down. When we're done, or she wants to leave, we'll make sure she gets home. At this point, there is no reason for us to believe she had anything to do with Mr. VanHoy's murder."

"What exactly do you mean, murder?" I asked. "What happened to VanHoy? What pictures? Are other people being questioned? What about the other business owners? Everyone is having the same 'altercation' with VanHoy right now. Are you talking to them?"

"Miss?" Detective Harrison said pointing at me, clearly inquiring my name.

"Culpepper. Treasure Culpepper."

"And you?" he asked pointing at Theodora.

"Theodora Culpepper," she responded.

"Sisters. How lovely," he said sarcastically, writing in a little notebook.

"Hello?" I said, trying to bring the conversation back to my questions, "what about Mrs. VanHoy? Is she okay?"

"She's fine. At the station," Travis said reassuringly.

"Okay, so what happened?" I asked again.

"Miss Culpepper, I cannot discuss an ongoing investigation with you. If you have questions, you can contact the Sheriff's Department Information Officer, since we're handling the investigation. He can provide you with any details that can be shared publicly."

"Why can't you just tell us the public details?" I asked.

"Because I'm not your personal liaison. You can get the information just like everyone else."

I rolled my eyes. "Okay, so what about the other business owners? Are you talking to them? Can I ask you that?"

"Aren't you a business owner?" Detective Harrison flipped a couple of pages in his notebook.

"Yes, we are. We own The Alchemist," I said pointing across the street.

"And were you here yesterday when Ms. Parker and Mr. VanHoy were arguing?"

"Yes," I responded.

"We all were," Theodora added. "And Mrs. VanHoy was in our shop when it happened."

"Hmm..." Detective Harrison mumbled while scribbling in his notebook.

"So, you all witnessed the argument?"

"Yes," I repeated.

"Well," he said smiling, "You ladies are welcome to join Ms. Parker and me this morning. There's plenty of room in the back seat."

Chapter 3

VanHoy was murdered. In the town square. Hit on the back of the head. Right among the pumpkins and holiday decorations. After several long hours at the police station, we piled into another government sedan to be taken back to The Alchemist. And despite our horror, it appeared by the direction the officer took from the parking lot, we were going to drive right by the crime scene.

As we reached the end of the street, the downtown area came into view. I heard Deidra gulp. Tara put on her sunglasses, and Theo gave us all a reassuring smile. A pit formed in my stomach as my heart began to race. After we turned the corner, the taped-off crime scene came into full view. We all craned our necks to get a better look. The only thing that seemed out of place was that a white pop-up tent had been erected, and a dozen or so individuals were meandering about. Eerily, if one hadn't known there had been an actual murder, the area seemed almost like it was staged. It fit in so well with the Halloween decorations. I shivered at the thought.

The ride from the Seven Hills police station back to The Alchemist took less than 5 minutes, but it felt like forever. None of us spoke. The morning had been absolutely exhausting, even though most of our time had been spent waiting around drinking sour coffee. Police coffee was definitely not Deidra's coffee, and I was looking forward to a fresh cup of her pumpkin-spice blend to get the bad taste out of my mouth. As we arrived at The Alchemist and crawled out of the car, I noticed several local shop owners and pedestrians took notice of our arrival. *Great, just great*, I thought to myself.

Deidra looked especially beat. Although she was finally cried out, the gravity of the situation was clearly weighing on her still.

"Come on," I said taking her arm, "let me take you home."

"No," she stated softly, "I need to get back to the bakery to see if the girls need anything. I'll be okay."

"Just go and stay with her, Treasure," Theodora said, searching for her business keys. "Tara and I will take care of things here."

I nodded, and Deidra and I walked across the street. When we entered Seven Sweets, several of the customers abruptly stopped talking and looked up. Deidra didn't seem to notice and continued walking to the kitchen. I made my way to the large booth in the back of the bakery and sat down.

"Hey Treasure," Maria, one of the waitresses said, as she placed a cup of coffee in front of me. "What's going on? Is it true? Was VanHoy murdered?"

I nodded my head yes as I took a sip of the coffee. With a look of concern, Maria stepped a little closer to the table so no one could hear. "Did Deidra...?"

"No!" I interrupted, a little louder than I would have liked. "Deidra had nothing to do with VanHoy's murder. The police were just here this morning to question her about their argument yesterday."

"Oh," Maria said looking to the ground. "It's just that...everyone keeps asking. A lot of people saw Deidra being taken out of the bakery this morning by the police. They said she was really upset."

"Yes, she's upset. But not because she did anything wrong. You tell anyone who asks that Deidra didn't have anything to do with VanHoy's murder. People need to mind their own business." I stated, raising my voice again.

A couple of people looked in my direction, and I smiled back. *Ah, the joys of living in Seven Hills*, I thought to myself.

Deidra emerged from the kitchen with a plate of chocolate cake, and Maria scurried back to the front counter. Plopping the plate of cake on the table, she handed me a fork and sat down.

"I don't think given the circumstances that it's too early for chocolate cake," Deidra said, taking a large bite.

"It's never too early for chocolate cake," I said, digging in with my fork. Deidra's chocolate cake was decadent. The rich-chocolate flavor wasn't overly sweet, and it just melted in your mouth.

"How are you feeling now?" I asked between bites.

"I really am doing better. I just couldn't believe what I was hearing this morning. When Travis and Detective Harrison showed up at the bakery, I was absolutely terrified that they thought I had something to do with this. Even though I heard them tell me that I wasn't a suspect, I feel like every crime movie I've ever watched starts with the cops telling the suspected murderer that they aren't a suspect."

Odd but true that so much of our perceptions of things were based on television. "Absolutely," I agreed. "So, what did they talk to you about?"

"Well, they asked a lot of questions about the Value Mart project and what VanHoy's been saying to me and others. I explained what happened yesterday, and I told Detective Harrison that I lost my temper and was practically pushing him out of the bakery. That's how we ended up in the street. What about you?"

I swallowed a bite of cake and took a sip of coffee.

"Mostly, the same. However, our position is much different because, in theory, we aren't going to be displaced by the store. But I'm sure, once construction begins and they start widening the street, we'll get pushed out too. VanHoy never came into The Alchemist. I think he was afraid we would put a hex on him!"

Deidra laughed which made me smile.

"It's going to be okay," I continued. "The police will figure out who did this. A lot of people were angry with VanHoy. That man made a lot of enemies."

"Yes, he did," Deidra replied, her voice trailing away.

"So," I continued. "Detective Harrison said he was going to show you some pictures. Did you recognize anyone?"

"Um, no, I didn't," She replied. "Honestly, I don't think I have ever seen any of those people before, so I don't think they're local. A couple were mug shots. They kind of looked like old-timey gangsters or something. I don't know."

"What was their connection to VanHoy?" I wondered aloud.

"I don't know," Deidra said, taking another bite of cake. "Detective Harrison didn't say."

"Interesting," I said curiously. "Do you think maybe Van Hoy was getting some sort of kick-back or something from Value Mart for pushing the store?"

"Kick-back?" Deidra said, raising her eyebrows. "Do you think we could be talking about some sort of conspiracy or something?"

"I don't know; just thinking out loud," I said, biting my lower lip. "VanHoy wasn't exactly known to be an upstanding citizen. And with you describing the people in the pictures as 'old-timey gangsters,' maybe this was something a bit more complicated. There's a lot of money riding on this deal," I said, continuing my train of thought. "Maybe VanHoy got in over his head."

"Who knows," Deidra said, shrugging her shoulders. "I'll be glad when all of this is over."

The Alchemist was especially busy. I'm sure some of the customers were people we would have seen anyway, but I was starting to get the feeling that many customers were dropping by just for curiosity's sake. I'm sure everyone who saw Deidra leaving with the police saw us too, but no one asked any questions. Around 4 o'clock, I heard Tara groan loudly. I looked up, and she nodded her head to the front door as Kristy Pickles walked in. I couldn't help but groan too.

Kristy Pickles was the most obnoxious gossip in Seven Hills. For Kristy, gossip and the town's goings-on were a sport. She was the commentator. We usually saw her about once or twice a week as she wandered around the downtown stores. She never made any purchases, but that never stopped her from asking a million and one questions about different products or offering suggestions about what products we should have in the store. Usually, she would just loiter and listen to other people's conversations. Then, she would hang out at the counter and recount everything she had learned about everyone else. I had little patience for that woman. Theo would usually handle all interactions with her, but I could tell from Theo's face that she wasn't in the mood.

"Good afternoon, girls," Kristy said, in her high-pitched, sing-songy voice. "It's a beautiful day. I noticed you opened later than usual. I hope everything's okay." Her voice was soaked in fake concern. I rolled my eyes.

"Everything's just fine here, Kristy," Theo said smiling. "How may we help you today?"

"Oh, I'm just browsing," she replied, running her fingers across some of the lotion bottles.

"Inventory hasn't changed in the last three days, Kristy," Tara said, walking over to her. "Maybe we don't have what you need."

"Well, you never know," she laughed nervously. "So, did you hear about Mr. VanHoy? How sad. I can't believe we all know someone who's been murdered. Isn't that so scary?"

We all stared at her. Of course, we knew VanHoy had been murdered. She knew that we knew. Of course, she also knew that we knew another person who had been murdered. *Allegedly murdered; missing,* I corrected myself, a black pit forming in my stomach. Kristy looked at each of us, and when we didn't respond, switched tactics.

"So, that Detective Mike Harrison is a real looker," she said, popping the lid off a lip balm to smell it. "I used to see him all the time at the pub with Lydia Swinger. You know Lydia, right Tara? Wasn't she in your class?" Tara didn't respond.

"Anyway," Kristy continued, "I think they dated for a while. Lydia obviously wanted more, and Mike obviously wouldn't commit. I heard that he had been dating several women while he was dating Lydia. Sounds like a real player. I thought for sure he'd be after Sarah. I'm sure he'll be after her next."

I had to roll my eyes. Kristy was Sarah's biggest fan. Kristy was Sarah's...lackey? I never understood their friendship. I remember once in high school at a party, Sarah slapped Kristy across the face so hard that it left a handprint. Kristy ended up apologizing to Sarah at the end of the night. At least that is how the story goes. I, of course, was not at said party. Theo and Tara were losing interest in Kristy, but hearing Detective Harrison's name piqued my interest. I moved closer to Kristy. I would probably regret asking later, but I couldn't help myself.

"So, is Detective Harrison from around here?" As soon as I asked, Kristy returned the lip balm and turned to face me. Her face lit up as she took as step closer.

"No, he's not," she began in a low voice. "He's from Boston. He worked for *the* Boston Police Department and evidently was some sort of big-shot detective over there...a homicide detective. Obviously, he was damaged by the cases he worked. That's probably why he wouldn't commit to Lydia. That's probably why he doesn't have the confidence to pursue Sarah. It's sad really, that someone so attractive could be so damaged on the inside."

Kristy placed her hand on her chest. I struggled not to roll my eyes; I could see Theodora shaking her head behind the counter.

"Anyway," Kristy continued, "I heard that he'd been working on a really big case. He messed up, and the guy walked. Some say Mike had something to do with the case falling apart. All I know for sure is, all of a sudden, he ended up at our county sheriff's office. I mean, who leaves Boston to move out here?" she asked rhetorically, swinging her arms out wide. "He must have done something wrong. That's the only thing that makes sense. So, why do you ask?"

"Well, we've seen him at work with the Seven Hills PD. I was just wondering," I said.

"I see," Kristy said, looking at me suspiciously. "Well, he is a homicide detective," she said, raking her eyes over my face.

"Yeah, makes sense," I said flatly, half returning my attention to her. Kristy smiled, walking away to chat with some other customers. I joined Theodora and Tara at the front counter.

"Why are you talking to her?" Tara demanded in a whisper. "You know she just wants to dig up dirt on what happened this morning!"

"Of course, I know!" I whispered back. "I'm just trying to get some information from her. We know everyone at Seven Hills PD, and for some reason, they brought in a county detective we've never seen to work the VanHoy case. Why is that?"

"I don't know," Theodora responded. "I hadn't really thought about it. They're all cops."

"I just think there's something else going on," I whispered. "And I'm concerned for Deidra. We don't know this detective. What if Kristy is right, and he is some disgraced Boston PD detective? Can we trust him?"

"We know we can't trust Kristy," Tara countered. "Think about some of the stuff she's said about us over the years."

"True," I acknowledged. Kristy didn't verify information before spreading it around. Her mouth had caused us some stress.

"Look," Theodora interjected, "I can't imagine Chief Dodd would allow Detective Harrison to come here if he thought Harrison was a bad cop."

Tara and I both nodded in agreement. Chief Dodd was a good man. He had always looked out for our family, even when it was difficult.

"She needs to go," Theodora said, pointing to the window.

Tara and I turned to see Kristy pointing at Seven Sweets, with several of the women in the shop looking in the pointed direction.

"I got this," Tara said, sprinting to the window.

"Oh," Theodora said with concern. "Treasure, maybe you should assist with that." Tara bounced right behind the group of women, startling several of them.

"Ladies," she said, in her best lunchroom monitor voice. "Are we shopping or are we gossiping? Because it doesn't look like we're shopping." Several of them opened their mouths to respond, but only a few mumbled sounds came out. "That's what I thought," Tara continued, raising her arms like she was directing a tour group. "And now, we're walking to the door. And we're walking, we're walking…," she said, following behind the women, shooing them with her hands. "Next time you're in, I recommend purchasing some of our new candles that Treasure has been working on. They are simply splendid."

Theodora and I looked in horror as the last woman exited the store. Tara turned to face Theodora and me, and Theodora shook her head disapprovingly.

"What?!" Tara asked, throwing up her arms. "I told them to come back for candles."

We hadn't been open very long the following morning, when I noticed a lot of extra foot traffic at Seven Sweets. At one point, the counter line was pushing out the front entrance. Seven Sweets had always been popular. Deidra was an absolute genius when it came to baked goods, so she got a lot of business from locals as well as tourists. But this amount of busy seemed unusual.

"Okay, what's the deal?" Theo said, looking out the window. "Don't get me wrong, I'm glad this whole thing hasn't impacted her business in a negative way, but something is clearly going on over there."

"We should go see if she needs any backup," Tara said, joining Theo at the window. "Seriously, maybe some of her girls are sick or something."

"Good point," I said, joining them.

"You two go over," Theodora said, heading back to the register. "I'm fine here. Just call if you need something. I'll close the store if she needs help."

Tara and I walked across the street to Seven Sweets. The line was still really backed up, and we had trouble getting in the front door. After pushing our way in, we could see all the normal waitresses busily assisting customers. Deidra usually had around three people working the bakery with her, but I counted three weekend shift waitresses as well. Looks like Deidra had already called in backup. Deidra busted through the swinging door from the kitchen to the front counter carrying a tray of muffins.

"Behind, behind!" she shouted, heading to the display case. Several of the waitresses plucked muffins from the tray before she could even get it inside.

"This is nuts!" I said to Tara. She nodded.

We made our way to the rear of the bakery and entered the kitchen. It was an absolute disaster. Deidra always kept a tidy kitchen, but things were obviously hectic today.

"Here," Tara said, handing me an apron. We both tied on aprons and got to work.

Tara started sweeping the floor as I wiped down the counters and began some dishes. We could see she was low on about every type of pastry, so I got the batter started just as Deidra exploded back into the kitchen. When she saw us, she immediately burst into tears. I ran over to her and wrapped my arms around her.

"Deidra, what's going on?" I asked, pulling back to look at her face.

"I am so overwhelmed," she exclaimed, "and coming back here and seeing you girls...thank you! I really needed that."

"Of course," I said. "We love you. You could have called us. We would have come over to help."

"You have your own business to run," she said, wiping her eyes.

"If you need help, you know we would shut down the store. and come over here. In fact, why don't I call Theo and tell her to come over?" I started to pull my phone out of my pocket, but Deidra stopped me.

"No, no, it's fine," she replied. "Cleaning the kitchen and starting this batter is a tremendous help. Maybe you could help with some other batters? If we could get some more things in the oven really quick, that would help me catch up." Deidra pulled a couple of recipes and handed them to Tara and me.

"I just don't understand why all of these people are here," she continued. "Some of these folks haven't been in the bakery in years."

"It's because they think you murdered VanHoy," Tara blurted out. Deidra stopped in her tracks, her bottom lip quivering.

"Tara!" I scolded.

"What?" she said, shrugging her shoulders. "Let's call this what it is—everyone is here because they think you murdered VanHoy. Plain and simple. Embrace it." I agreed with Tara's assessment—it did seem like everyone was there to gawk, but I wish Tara hadn't said it like that.

"Embrace what?" Deidra shrieked, tears flowing again.

"All of that coin you're going to make from these stupid people," Tara declared, with her hands on her hips. "Raise the prices now! Today, that $3 muffin is going to cost you $5, thank you very much. Just think of it as compensation for that asshole causing you all this drama by getting himself murdered and threatening your business. And let them talk! If you want, Treasure and I can head to the dining room and start talking about being questioned by the police in a *real loud voice*!" Tara continued, raising her voice by several octaves at the end of her sentence.

We all paused when the rumblings of conversations noticeably hesitated in the dining room for a couple of seconds.

"See," Tara said, pointing at the door. "Embrace it."

"Argh!" Deidra exhaled loudly and raised her hands to her face. "I can't do this," she said in a near whisper. "I couldn't sleep last night; I'm having nightmares. I can hear people whispering my name, and others stop talking when I come over to their table. I'm feeling all of this pressure," she said, clutching her chest. "I know it's only been a day, but I really need for this to be over. What if Detective Harrison can't solve this case? What if it drags on for months? What if-"

I cut her off.

"Deidra! This case will be solved; I promise you. We will do everything in our power to help you get through this. We will do whatever needs to be done."

"Thank you," Deidra exhaled, wrapping Tara and I both into a hug. "I hope I don't sound insensitive…to…you know…. Anyway, I seriously couldn't do this without you!"

One of the waitresses pushed through the swinging door and stopped when she saw us.

"Oh, I'm sorry," she stammered, taking a step back.

"It's okay, Penny," Deidra said, releasing her embrace. "What do you need?"

"Help up here," she said timidly.

"I got this," Tara said, heading to the door. Deidra gave me a concerned look.

"She has this," I said, shrugging my shoulders. "Just stay in the back. I'll help you get these other recipes going." Deidra nodded. She started to walk away but paused.

"Do you seriously think I should raise my prices?" she asked, barely moving her lips.

"Oh, Tara is definitely doing that right now," I said, shaking my head, "so you don't even have to worry about it. Shall we make some scones?"

"Yes," she said smiling. "Let's make some scones!"

Closing time at Seven Sweets brought welcomed relief. Tara shooed the remaining costumers out of the bakery and promptly locked the door. With the extra waitresses, cleaning the main dining room and kitchen areas was done in record time. Tara and I hugged Deidra goodbye and walked back to The Alchemist.

Theodora greeted us at the front door. "How did it go?" she asked.

"Exhausting!" Tara exclaimed. She dropped into our favorite plaid wingback chair in the corner of the shop.

"We got her all caught up," I explained. "We have some things prepped for tomorrow. I think it'll start to calm down."

Tara snorted.

"Fat chance of that," she said, kicking off her shoes. "Even when they catch the murderer, Deidra has been branded. That's what happens around here. It's not like the police will publicly clear her name. She should just hire more staff now."

Theo and I exchanged worried glances. Tara was right about Deidra being branded. Once it happens in Seven Hills, it tends to stick with you. Our family was proof of that. We had managed to deal with the whispers and comments over the years, but Deidra was different. Our family had historically been on the margins of society, so we had been raised to deal with it. Deidra never had to worry about any of that.

"What do we do?" Theo asked us.

"We stay on top of the police," I said. "In fact, I think I'll go over tomorrow and check on the status of the investigation. Maybe even talk with Chief Dodd."

Early the next morning, I woke abruptly to my ringing cell phone.

"Hello?" I said groggily.

"Treasure!" Deidra said between sobs. Hearing Deidra's voice caused me to sit straight up in bed.

"Deidra? What's wrong?" Deidra attempted to speak several times, but she was not able to get the words out.

"It's okay," I said, ignoring my pounding heart. "Take your time. Take a deep breath." I heard Deidra take a couple of deep breaths; then she cleared her throat.

"Someone spray-painted 'Murderer' on the front of Seven Sweets," she sniffled. "It's in red paint. On the front window."

"What?!" I shrieked, jumping out of bed. I looked at the clock on my bedside table; it was 3:45 am, so Deidra was surely there alone. "Deidra, get out of the bakery and go to The Alchemist. Use your key, let yourself in, and lock the door behind you. Did you call the police?"

"No," she cried.

"Just leave the bakery. Do you want me to call the police?"

"No, no, I'll do it," she said, sniffling. "Can you come?"

"I'm already on my way," I said, pulling on some jeans with one hand. "I'm going to stay on the phone with you until you are locked in The Alchemist."

"Okay, I'm going right now." I listened to Deidra as she exited the bakery and hurried across the street. I ran out of my room and into Tara's. She was already coming out of her bedroom, pulling on a sweatshirt.

"I could hear you yelling through the wall," she said in an annoyed voice, grabbing her sunglasses. "I'll get Theo. You go get the car started."

I ran down the steps and grabbed my purse and car keys.

"Deidra?" I asked into the phone.

"Almost in," she answered. "My hands are shaking so bad I can't get my key into the door."

"Take a moment and breathe," I coached. "You can do this."

"I got it!" she exclaimed. I heard the rear door of The Alchemist open, and slam shut.

"Good! Now hang up and call the police. We're on our way!"

We made it to The Alchemist in record time. Two Seven Hills police cruisers were in front of the bakery. Even though it was still dark, I could clearly see 'Murderer' spray painted across the window of Seven Sweets, brightly illuminated by the light coming from the bakery. I jumped out of my car and hustled to the back door of The Alchemist. The door was open, and Deidra was talking with Travis, who had a hand on her shoulder.

"Deidra!" I yelled, "Are you okay?"

"I'm okay," she said, obviously calmer since our phone call. "Travis and Jimmy walked through the bakery, and said they didn't think anyone broke in."

"Yeah," Travis continued, "all of the doors were locked. There was no sign of a break-in. It just looks like the vandalism was limited to the outside window."

"Thank goodness," Theo said from the back door.

"Obviously this is related to VanHoy," I started. "Why else would Deidra be targeted?"

"I'm sure it's related to all of the attention from the case," Travis agreed, "but I really don't think there's any danger here. It was probably just kids."

"Okay, but still," I pressed, "what's going on with the investigation? Clearly Deidra has become a target."

"You know how everyone gossips 'round here," Travis answered. "I'm sure that's all this is."

"You're missing the point, Travis," Tara piped in from the back. "We understand that this was probably done by a couple of punk kids, but what are you going to do about it?"

"Right. People obviously think Deidra had something to do with this. Next time, it may not be kids." I added.

"What do you want me to do?" Travis asked. "Search every teenager for red spray paint?"

"Uhm, yah," Tara said, stepping forward.

"And what's going on with the investigation?" I asked again.

"Guys, I can't talk about the case," Travis said, shaking his head.

"Come on, Travis!" Tara said, raising her voice.

"Seriously, Tara," Travis said, putting his hands on his duty belt. "We can't talk about an ongoing investigation."

"Seriously?" Tara grunted loudly, while rolling her eyes. "What are you good for?!"

"Travis, can you just tell us if there is a suspect?" I asked.

"No," he said, shaking his head, "I can't tell you. You need to let this play out."

"Meanwhile, Deidra is getting her bakery vandalized while you 'let this play out.'" Tara said, putting her hands on her hips. "Are you even going to investigate it?"

Just then, Jimmy Dickson, the other officer at the bakery, walked into the back of The Alchemist.

"Great," Tara exclaimed sarcastically, "Barney Fife's on the case!" Jimmy gave Tara a side-eye glance, ignoring her comment.

"Deidra, I took some pictures. You can clean the paint off."

"Okay," Deidra responded. "What happens next?"

"We'll make a report," Travis explained.

"And then what?" I asked.

"Then, if we hear something, we'll let you know," Travis said, shrugging his shoulders. "There's really not much we can do here."

"Are you at least going to tell Detective Harrison?" I asked. "Shouldn't he know?"

"I really don't think this is serious, Treasure," Travis said.

"Are you serious?!" I pressed on; "how do you know that?"

"You girls seem awfully set on making a big deal out of a little red paint," Jimmy chimed in. "Maybe someone here painted the window to get our attention?"

"WHAT?!" we all screamed. Jimmy's eyes went wide, and he took a step back.

"I...I...well, did you?" he stuttered.

"Why on earth would we do that, Dickson?" Tara growled. "The last thing any of us needs in this inbred little town is negative attention!"

My whole body trembled as tensions climbed rapidly in the close quarters. I could see my sisters steaming as well, clearly reaching a breaking point. Just as we all nearly exploded in anger, Detective Harrison walked in the rear door.

"Mornin' ladies," he said way too cheerfully. "I heard you had a problem at the bakery, Ms. Parker, so I wanted to stop in myself before heading to the police station this morning. Are you okay?"

Detective Harrison's question clearly knocked all of us off-guard, causing a much-needed pressure release from the room.

"Yeah...Um...yeah, I'm okay...," Deidra stammered.

"Look, I went over and viewed the damage. Looks like everything is limited to the outside. Did you see any signs of a break-in?" he asked, directing his question to Travis and Jimmy.

"No, sir" Travis said. "Everything was locked up tight."

"Okay. We'll look at it again in the daylight just to make sure. Sometimes it's difficult to see evidence of minor tool marks with flashlights," he explained to Deidra. "I know this is upsetting, but it looks to me like this was done by kids." Again, directing his attention to Jimmy and Travis, "Get with the other businesses on this street that have surveillance cameras and pull the footage from last night."

Jimmy's eyebrows raised, and he gave Travis a perplexed look.

"Um, footage? For some tagging?" he said, chuckling.

"Yes," Detective Harrison admonished, "for some tagging. Do you have a problem with that, Officer Dickson?"

"Um, no. No, sir," Jimmy choked, shooting a quick glance towards his partner. Travis slightly shrugged as they both headed for the door. Detective Harrison watched them leave, and then redirected his attention to Deidra.

"We are going to look into this because I don't want this escalating into anything else," the detective said assuredly. "But again, I really believe this was done by kids, and I don't think you're in any danger."

"Thank you," Deidra replied, clearly relieved. Detective Harrison seemed sincere in his assessment, and even if the incident was not related to VanHoy's murder, it was nice that he at least was taking it seriously.

After a couple moments of silence, I asked Detective Harrison, "okay, so now what?"

"The officers will make a report, and I'll have them follow up with anything found on the footage," He replied. "We will also pay attention to all the social media. Typically, chatter for something like this travels quickly. I'm sure we'll be able to figure out who is responsible. Once we get a suspect, we can discuss what you want to do, Ms. Parker. You can decide to press charges, or we can try something more informal, like perhaps having the kids clean the bakery." We all nodded.

"What's going on with the VanHoy investigation?" I asked a third time. "Being called a 'murderer' is clearly related to that incident. Is there a suspect in that case?"

"Miss Culpepper," Detective Harrison began, annoyance starting to creep into his face. "I can't discuss the investigation. I agree that the word spray-painted on the window is definitely related to what happened to Mr. VanHoy, but these are separate incidents."

"But-" I couldn't get another word out before Detective Harrison interrupted me.

"Let me do my job," he stated firmly. "I'm the detective, okay," he stated, pointing to himself.

"You," he continued, pointing to the four of us, "are not detectives. My job is to investigate. Your job is to stay out of it."

Detective Harrison's speech became laced with sarcasm and condescension, just as it was the first day we met him. Any possible redeeming qualities I thought for a moment that he might possess, given his kindness to Deidra when he first walked in, evaporated immediately. I audibly sighed. He looked at me with a raised eyebrow, clearly waiting for a rebuttal. I did not speak.

"Okay then," he said, smirking. "Ms. Parker, you'll be hearing from Seven Hills PD when they have more information."

And with that, Detective Harrison slowly turned around and coolly walked out the rear door.

We all stood there, stunned for a moment. Panic tended to come in waves; it crept up and subsided, jostling you, sickening you, and keeping you off-balance in the process. I felt so exhausted, I could barely stand. The word *weary* came to my mind.

"Do you really think that someone could be trying to throw police attention towards us?" Tara asked softly. "You know with the spray paint...." Her voice trailed off. "Or, could this be just 'kids having fun' or whatever."

I looked at her. She was so young when Jasper Alden, our father, disappeared. I realized that she was probably the most impacted by his disappearance. Theo, Tara, and I didn't have much of a relationship with our father. He had lived in Seven Hills until the day he *disappeared*. Yet, we barely knew him. Sometimes, while growing up, it had seemed so foreign to me that I even had a father. It was almost like my Mom and Aunt Elaina cooked us up; they made a potion, and there we were. They were my parents. Not Jasper.

Although Tara was young when Jasper...*left*?, she had to grow up in a place where the police eyed us, and where old friends had turned on us. She blamed our Mom for putting us in that position. She blamed our Mom for dying. No wonder she had to leave this place. I am surprised she ever came back.

"No, of course not," I said, my voice barely a whisper.

"I'm so sorry," Deidra said, slumping into a chair. She held her head in her hands.

"Deidra, this is not your fault. You did not do anything wrong. I bet this is just a couple of young kids, being terrible," Theo said, her voice measured.

"It just always feels like people are so suspicious of you all—" Deidra began. Theo visibly winced as she cut off Deidra's words. If she did not say them, perhaps they were not real.

"I know," Theo countered. "I know."

Chapter 4

I set out in my car along State Route 2. The morning was oppressively dark. There was no moon and no stars in the cloudy black sky. I blinked my dry eyes again and again, trying desperately to produce some moisture. The events of the last couple of days had caught up with me, and, with the car heater going, I was having trouble staying awake. I was thankful it was not a long drive. The last thing I needed was to fall asleep on this dark, winding road. I thought about stopping at a gas station in town to grab some coffee but felt too exhausted to even get out of the car.

I pulled into the alley alongside The Alchemist. As I opened the car door, the wind whipped around me, smelling of falling leaves and morning dew. The faint smell of cinnamon wafted over from Seven Sweets. I breathed in deeply, filling my lungs with the scent. There was no one around, and it was quite peaceful. It was also a little creepy. I could not help but think about the man, or woman, who had attacked VanHoy and the vandals who had spray-painted 'murderer' on the window of Seven Sweets. I knew that these likely were not the same people. Yet, I still imagined him or her lurking behind every corner, muscles tensed like a panther's, ready to strike. My heart racing, I quickly unlocked The Alchemist door and headed to the back, uncharacteristically locking it behind me. My body ached as I made the walk. All the rolling, kneading, and running around at Seven Sweets yesterday made me sore today. I made a silent pact with myself to start back at the gym on Monday. *How was it that I was so out of shape that a bit of baking kicked my ass?* I had to stay focused though; I had a plan for today. I left a note on the kitchen counter at home this morning for Theo and Tara, telling them that I had already left for the shop. I left another note for them on The Alchemist register counter, explaining that I had left for deliveries. It was too early to text. Based on the night we had all endured, I did not want to wake them up any earlier than absolutely necessary. Anyway, we needed to drive separately today in order to make all of the deliveries, as the All Hallows' Eve Parade and Pageant were approaching rapidly. The festivities were now just days away.

By 7:30 am, my sore body had loaded all the boxes. Soon, Theo and Tara would be at The Alchemist. I locked the door and got back into my car, suddenly regretting having made this batch of candles, as the boxes were very heavy. I turned the key in the ignition and began driving. I knew where I was headed: Seven Hills Town Hall. I wanted to get there early to be the first to talk with Nancy Miller. She would surely know the whereabouts of VanHoy on the day he was murdered. Perhaps, if I got answers to a few questions, I would better understand what was happening in Seven Hills. Then, I could extricate all of us from this mess.

I pulled into the town hall parking lot and parked in a spot in front of the building. Seven Hills Town Hall looked less like a government building and more like another old colonial. My car was one of three; no doubt, the other two belonged to security guards, who shortly would be opening the building. Perhaps, one of the cars was even Nancy's. As I waited, I reclined my seat and closed my eyes. *Did I even have time to rest my eyes for a bit?* The stress, sore muscles, and car heater were proving to be a deadly combination. I tried to keep my eyes open and think of how I would ask Nancy about VanHoy's schedule. I needed to know how to frame these questions so that it did not seem odd or suspicious. I was not sure how much time had passed when I heard a knock on my window. I must have dozed off.

"Whoa!" I yelled, my eyes popping open and my body surging with adrenaline.

"I'm sorry. I'm sorry," a man repeated, stepping back from my car, his hands up in a submissive pose.

I peered out the window, and my eyes began to focus. The man was impeccably dressed in brown slacks and a tweed-fitted jacket.

"Ronnie?" I stammered, attempting to roll down my window. Then, giving up, I just opened my door, "Ronnie?" I asked again, as if to verify.

"Treasure!" he said excitedly, a broad smile unfolding across his boyish face. "What are you doing here so early?" he asked laughing.

"Can't a girl sleep in a parking lot anymore?" I asked, his demeanor putting me at ease. I mustered a half-hearted smile.

"Are you waiting for someone?" he asked.

"Nancy," I said. "I'm hoping to talk with her."

"Do you want to wait in my office?" he asked. He paused and then added, like he was attempting to close a sale, "I have a coffee machine."

I smiled broadly and happily nodded. "Yes, that would be great. You have an office in town hall?" I asked, grabbing my bag.

I made sure to hit the lock on the door, as if someone would want my old clunker. *God, we are all so cheap*, I thought to myself. I felt slightly embarrassed around Ronnie. I knew he had some money. Everyone in town knew of his success. His jacket, his slacks, even his brain, filled with information from Harvard—everything about him was expensive, yet dignified, not flashy.

"I have a grant through the state," he said. "There was a vacant office, and the town offered it to me. It's nice because I don't have to commute back and forth to the university to work."

"Nice," I responded, nodding.

Suddenly, I did not know what to say to this man with whom I had grown up. Apart from brief encounters at the library, I tried to think of the last time we had a real conversation. *Maybe ten years ago?* I did not remember much of Ronnie from high school. I remembered that he was a nice, smart guy, but I was not interested in him. In fact, I did not recall anybody being interested, although I am not sure why.

"I've wanted to get in touch with you," he said, unlocking the front door to the building.

"Really?" I said in disbelief. "Why?" I asked curtly, immediately regretting the tone of my voice. Ronnie let out a jovial laugh.

"I'm interested in you," he said, then actually turned a bit red. He smiled shyly and attempted to correct himself, "...interested in your *family*."

A pit suddenly formed in my stomach. My family was interesting, maybe too interesting. *What could he be interested in?*

"Oh, really?" was all I could think to say.

"Yes, I'm interested in all of the historic families," he said smiling, putting me at ease.

I took a breath. *This is a research project*, I reminded myself. *This was not another investigation.* He unlocked the door and ushered me into his office.

"Did you know that you are related to Sarah Culpepper? There is a record of her living here all the way back to the 1690s. Surely, you must have known this."

"Oh," I laughed, feeling the last residuals of tension leaving my body.

His light energy made me feel safe, and he was clearly excited about the history. He seemed as giddy as a schoolboy. Delight was written all over this face as he searched through some of his materials before snatching a big, leather-bound book off one of the shelves and plopping it on his desk. He immediately started flipping through the pages.

"Sarah Culpepper was accused of Witchcraft. It's a matter of public record," he said, smiling brilliantly.

My guard went back up a bit. "Oh," was all I could seem to mutter.

"She was accused but found innocent," he explained. "This was super interesting and rare for this time period. Almost no woman—or man for that matter—was ever accused of Witchcraft, found innocent, and lived. It is quite extraordinary. Local lore posits that she was the only actual witch, meaning someone who practiced Witchcraft, who was tried and found innocent. She is believed to be the only *actual* witch of Seven Hills. Some believe that she worked her, you know, magic to set herself free."

Ronnie stopped talking and his eyes seemed to linger on me. I struggled to think of something to say. I felt uncomfortable, almost as if he was doing more than just looking at me; I was being *outed.* Of course, I knew about Sarah Culpepper. Every woman in my family knew about Sarah Culpepper. Apparently, I no longer knew words, but I knew about Sarah Culpepper. I even knew what she did to get that innocent verdict, and I shuddered at the thought. It involved a cow tongue in a black velvet purse, beneath a judge's chair. I wondered suddenly if Ronnie knew this. *That would add some spice to his research,* I thought.

He spoke again with kindness in his voice. "I envy your family's rich heritage. You should be proud. I'm working on tracing your family line all the way back to England, which has a rich history of Witchcraft. The name Culpepper means 'pepper gather.' It is likely that your family were herbalists, or alchemists, as far back as the 1500s. Once I have more information, I'll pass it along to you."

I nodded, again unable to find words. As he sat down, he motioned for me to have a seat in front of his desk. Suddenly, I felt like a student again, uncomfortable, talking with the principal. Although I was not a poor student, I did not love school. I loved creating. I loved working with nature. I loved when those outside of my family pretended that they hadn't heard the lore about my family, past or present.

"So, why are you meeting with Nancy?" he asked.

"Nancy?" I said, quizzically.

He laughed, "Yes. You told me in the parking lot that you were meeting with Nancy."

"Oh yes..." I said, my voice trailing off. *What should I say about this?*

"She's probably here already. I could walk you to the front desk," he offered.

I rose from my chair, "No, I'll be fine—"

"Please, Treasure, let me walk you there. It's just down the hall. You and I should really catch up sometime. I would love to take you to lunch...or dinner..." he said, sheepishly.

I wondered exactly what it was that we would be catching up on; I did not think we shared many common childhood memories, nor did I want to talk about my family history. Yet, he seemed so nice and genuine that I had to agree. I even smiled.

"That would be nice," I said, smiling again.

He stood up from the desk chair, pushing it in with his large, elegant hands, and we began walking down the hallway. Nancy was at her desk; she looked up and smiled tiredly when she saw us.

"Dr. Jackman and...Treasure? Is that you, Treasure? How are you honey?" She came out from around her desk and gave me a hug. Her perfume seemed to envelop me. She pulled back and grabbed my arms.

"Wow," she said, then looked at Ronnie for confirmation, "she is just as beautiful as ever. I always thought you were the most beautiful woman in Seven Hills."

I laughed. "Oh, please."

"I would have to agree," Ronnie said, with a shy smile.

I looked at him, and he looked suddenly at the floor.

"Can I help you both with something?" Nancy asked, returning to her desk.

"Treasure had a question," Ronnie said, gesturing towards me.

Suddenly, I realized that I did not know what to say. Between the nap and talking with Ronnie, I had not thought this through.

"I wondered if you could tell me a little about Mr. VanHoy," I said hesitantly.

Nancy looked like someone struck her, and I winced.

"Mayor VanHoy?" she exclaimed, horrified. "You know what happened, right?"

"I know. I do...I was going to ask...I was hoping to get some details about his schedule," I stammered. "What his activities were...you know...regarding work on the pageant."

Ronnie interjected, "Treasure and I are working on an article about the All Hallows' Eve Pageant. We were hoping to feature Mayor VanHoy's involvement, as a way to pay tribute to him and the history of this town."

I looked over at Ronnie, my mouth falling open. I moved to say something, but again the words would not come. Nancy looked at both of us and paused for what seemed like a minute. She then seemed to accept this explanation and began typing away on the computer, her long, red, acrylic nails clanking on the keyboard.

"Well," Nancy said, looking at her screen. "I know Mayor VanHoy wasn't the most popular person, but he certainly kept busy. Up until the day he...ahem...died; he was working tirelessly. I am looking at his iCalendar now. It looks like, on that day, he had planned to stop in town in the morning. His schedule indicated that he would be out of the office from 8 to 10 am. Then, he had appointments with Sarah Tarleton and John Martin. Sarah is involved with the pageant."

I nodded vigorously, putting the information in my phone.

"Thank you so much," I said enthusiastically. "I will talk with Sarah."

Nancy looked a bit uneasy, "I am here to help."

Neither Ronnie nor I said a word as he walked me to my car. We stopped when we got there, and he turned to look at me, studying me.

"I have to ask. Why do you need information about VanHoy's schedule?"

I paused, searching for the words. I opened my mouth to speak, but all I could manage to say was, "have you ever been to Seven Sweets?"

A half hour later, Ronnie and I were seated with Deidra at Seven Sweets, several cups of coffee deep into the conversation. The whole story had been relayed—the fight with VanHoy, the police-station interrogations, and the vandalism. He did not seem at all surprised by my attempts to find out information about VanHoy and the murder. In fact, he seemed excited by it. Deidra and I were both shocked when he mentioned that he would like to help.

"Do you remember anything about the day that VanHoy was murdered?" Deidra asked Ronnie, setting down a plate fixed with raspberry scones, pumpkin muffins with pepitas baked into the top, brownies laced with rich chocolate chips, and lemon bars dusted with powdered sugar.

I interrupted before Ronnie could respond. "Are you trying to kill us?" I asked, nodding towards the enormous plate of baked goods.

She laughed, "Well, if you don't eat them, Ronnie can take them with him." She turned to Ronnie and added, "I can't believe you haven't been in here before!"

Ronnie had taken a large bite of a chocolate brownie. "Oh, I'll be in regularly from now on," he said with a laugh. Then, turning serious, "The day

VanHoy was murdered, Hansen Mills was in town hall several times."

"Hansen Mills?" I asked. I recognized the name but little more.

"He's a local bar owner. He owns The Witches Brew right here in town. VanHoy's office is down the hall from mine, and I could smell Mills whenever he went by. He reeks like cigarettes and stale beer, a walking hangover. I don't know what they would discuss. I just know he would come into VanHoy's office quite regularly. Odd that Nancy did not mention Mills when we asked her about VanHoy's schedule. Perhaps, whenever he came in, it was unscheduled?"

"Hmmm. That is interesting. Maybe he was trying to persuade Mills to sell The Witches Brew like he was Deidra with Seven Sweets?"

"The Witches Brew is way across town though. It is nowhere close to the Value Mart project," Ronnie retorted.

"That's true," Deidra said. "So why was he there?"

"I think that's worth checking out. What business could Mills have had with VanHoy that would make him regularly come in and out of his office, especially without an appointment?" I wondered aloud. "I doubt that they were drinking buddies."

After a couple of minutes, we all decided to get back to work. Ronnie left to return to his office, Deidra went back to helping customers, and I went back to my car. Before anything else, I had to get today's deliveries done. Theo would kill me if I didn't. Luckily, I had a delivery to Sarah Tarleton. I drove through town, my fatigue from the morning now replaced with a sugar- and-caffeine-laced high. The weather was beautiful– crisp and cool. I rolled down my window and breathed deeply.

Sarah Tarleton and her committee must have been hard at work for days. The gazebo in the middle of the town square was in the process of a complete transformation. It looked like the many people working on it were turning the gazebo into a gigantic spider. There were men and women nailing together wooden boards from the roof that looked like large, menacing, arachnid legs. I tried to picture what this would be like when completed, but the full vision would not quite come. A gigantic sign hung from light post to light post that read, "All Hallows' Eve Parade and Pageant: October 31st." The festivities were only five days away.

I parked my car on the street and dashed towards the gazebo. The sounds of hammering and shouting filled my ears. There were supplies everywhere: paint, decorations, and even racks of clothes hanging in the gazebo. The lawn was littered with boxes, many unopened. I shifted the two boxes I carried in my arms and asked a volunteer if he knew where Sarah was. An older-looking man with a beard and tool belt pointed to Sarah, crouched by a table, ripping through a large cardboard box.

"Sarah," I called out cheerfully, walking over to her.

"Oh hey, Treasure," she said, barely bothering to look up from her task. "How are you?"

"Good," I said, shifting from one foot to the other. "I have your orders. Where do you want them?"

"Makeup, primer, and all that should go in the gazebo by the clothes racks," she answered quickly.

I shifted again, not making a motion to walk to the gazebo. "I was wondering if you had a minute."

She looked exhausted. She stood, "Not really," she said, not unkindly. "What's up?"

"I wondered if you could tell me a bit about the pageant and VanHoy's involvement in it," I stated matter-of-factly.

She finally looked up from the box, her pretty faced etched with something I could not quite read. In front of me was the actual prettiest woman in town, I thought as I remembered the comment made by Nancy and Ronnie. Sarah stood up, brushing her hands on her jeans.

"VanHoy is an asshole," she said, wearily, almost matter-of-factly. "I mean *was*. Of course, no one deserves to be murdered, but he really was an asshole, right?"

"You're right," I said and nodded in solidarity.

"VanHoy himself was not helping at all with the pageant. He was trying to shut the pageant down. Some crap about budgets or something. I don't know. I barely ever listened to him. I don't know why Mrs. VanHoy ever married him. I love Mrs. VanHoy. She was helping me every single day until this happened. She said if her husband cut the budget for the pageant, she would make sure he paid for it out of his own pocket. I guess this shut him up. You know how Mrs. VanHoy loves tradition and all of the All Hallows' Eve celebrations. I don't know why he would try to take this from her. Even after he didn't get his way, he was always here...just lurking around and scowling," she sighed. "He was like a petulant child. I guess it's wrong to speak ill of the dead, right?"

"Did he ever threaten you?" I asked.

Sarah eyed me suspiciously and seemed to think over the question and why I was asking it. She decided to answer, "Not in so many words. But he didn't concern me. I always had Mrs. VanHoy here to protect me. She sort-of fought the battles for me. Why do you ask?"

Sarah always had someone to fight the battles for her, I though grimly. Maybe I was jealous.

"I don't know; he threatened Deidra more than once. I guess I was curious if others had similar experiences with him," I said, nonchalantly. "And…it is bad luck to speak ill of the dead. It can create a vengeful spirit…or so they say."

"He already was a vengeful spirit," Sarah said unconcerned and sighed.

I nodded and walked away. I put the boxes of homemade cosmetics with the racks of clothes. As I walked to my car, the wind picked up, and I shuddered. This was all so *eerie*. I did not like VanHoy, but I hadn't wished him dead. I turned back to see Sarah holding up a ladder for another volunteer that I did not recognize. Then, I recalled the image of Kristy's red and blotchy face after a slap from her best friend. *Friends did the dirty work, or they were punished.* I shuddered again.

"Treasure!" I heard my name being called.

I turned to see Kristy walking towards me, waving her arms. It was almost as if I had conjured her. She smiled brightly. Fake. She wore a trendy outfit and had perfectly manicured hair and eyebrows.

"How are Deidra and the girls?" she asked, once she caught up with me.

"They are fine," I said curtly.

"Oh," she said, and I turned to walk away. She quickly followed. "It's just that I heard her shop was vandalized."

"Kristy," I retorted crossly, whirling around to look her fully in the face, my face just a foot from hers. She took a step back, looking as dumbfounded as a child being scolded. Her perfectly made-up face formed into a pout.

"You can't believe everything you hear," I snapped, and then I turned and began walking away again. This time at a faster clip.

"I know. I know," she stammered, continuing to follow me. In a perverse way, you had to admire her persistence. I finally reached the sidewalk, a bit out of breath when I noticed a burly man unpacking boxes.

"Is that Cliff Bishop?" I asked, stopping so fast that Kristy nearly crashed into me.

"Yes," she answered, more words forming on her lips.

"What is he doing here?" I asked, cutting her off before she could speak again. "I'm surprised he would participate in this."

Kristy laughed, "He does anything that Sarah says."

I turned and looked at Cliff, the hometown hero. He wore boot-cut jeans and a white shirt so tight that you could see the outline of every muscle of his fit body. *What would it be like to have a man like this do everything you said?*

"I have to go," I said, resuming my hasty exit.

I slowed my pace when I realized Kristy was no longer following me. I was so lost in my thoughts that I did not notice when a basic late model sedan pulled up beside me. The window rolled down slowly to reveal Detective Harrison. He looked at me and grinned broadly. He had a handsome smile, but the smile of a predator. A one thousand tooth smile. A shark's smile.

"Miss Culpepper. Care for a ride?" He said cheerfully. Of course, it wasn't a Mrs. VanHoy cheerful. It was a fake cheerful, a mocking cheerful. A satirical, "aren't small town people friendly," cheerful.

"Am I under arrest?" I asked, trying to match his cheerfulness.

"Not yet," he said in sing-song voice. Then, sterner, he added, "Get in."

I looked around and got in his car. This was exactly what children were taught not to do. You do not enter the car of a man with a shark smile.

"I drove over here," I said.

Ignoring me, he asked, "Do you like McDonald's?"

"No," I replied curtly.

"I like to get my coffee from there," he mused.

"Great," I responded.

"Why don't you ride with me? I've been wanting to talk to you."

"If you wanted to talk about coffee, I know about a million places in Seven Hills that will give you a better cup," I said, looking out the window.

His car smelled good. I wondered faintly what the smell was. It was woodsy—mahogany maybe?

"I like boring coffee" he said. "I'm a homicide detective. I like to be bored. Being bored means, nobody died."

I said nothing and looked over at him. He was impeccably dressed. It was almost exciting to be in his car. I wondered what it would be like to be in his car under different circumstances. I wondered what it would be like to be one of the many, according to Kristy, women who went out on dates with him. *What could this man possibly be like on a date?*

His fake jovialness returned, "so, I heard you are writing an article." He paused for what seemed like hours. "It's funny. I didn't know you were a writer."

He looked like the cat that ate the canary. *Gotcha.* He actually smiled to himself, as if this was the funniest joke anyone had told him all day.

"I dabble in a lot of different things," I said, again as bright as I could muster. This was apparently the little game we play. We were both just so damn cheerful. "I dislike being bored."

He grinned again, stroking the bit of black stubble that grew on his face and chin. He seemed to consider my statement and nodded as he pulled into the McDonald's drive thru.

"Want anything?" he asked, his blue eyes flashing, looking over at me.

"No," I responded, a bit nervously.

I wondered why I was here. Maybe he was going to arrest me. Perhaps, the killer was trying to frame Deidra or frame us, the Culpepper girls. The strange girls who lived on the edge of town. *They were all in a coven together*, I imagined people would whisper. *They wanted blood.* We sat for a few moments in silence, waiting for his order. His face was completely blank. He knew how to reveal nothing in moments of silence.

"Miss Culpepper, I understand you are concerned for your friend. But getting involved with a homicide investigation is not a smart idea. I need you, and everyone else involved, to trust me, those who work for me, and in the process."

"Of course..." I said. "I do."

"You don't," he said and laughed softly. "It's obvious you don't. Your sister even called one of my guys Barney Fife. He tattled to me as soon as we left your place."

"Tara says a lot of things. They do not necessarily reflect the views of our entire family," I said, I guess on the behalf of the Culpepper sisters.

"Why are you looking into VanHoy's activities?" he asked suddenly.

"I'm working on an article..." I began, but weakly.

"You are not working on an article," he countered, cutting me off. "I thought you were a...you know..." he paused for the right words, "...a local business owner."

A laugh burst from my lips, "you thought I was a...you know...a witch?"

"I just didn't think that you were a writer," he said with measured confidence. The corners of his mouth were upturned in a slight smile.

"I have many accomplishments and so does my family. I see, some of which you have obviously heard," I said, matching his tone.

He laughed then. "Yes, so it would seem."

He took a couple of bills from a very expensive wallet and handed them through the drive-thru window. He put his cup of coffee in the center console's cupholder. It was very strange to see such a well-dressed man at a McDonald's buying coffee. It seemed he should be sipping coffee out of a tiny, elegant cup at a trendy bistro in Italy or France.

"I'll take you back to your car."

He didn't touch his coffee as we drove. I began to suspect he wasn't actually going to drink the cup of black liquid. He drove me right up to my car, parked near the gazebo downtown.

"So, we have an understanding?"

"I understand what you are telling me," I said.

He looked at me, a smile on his face. But there was slight annoyance underneath the smile, as he understood that my statement was not actually an agreement.

As I exited the car, he called, "So, what does the name Treasure mean, exactly?"

I popped my head back into the still-open car door and responded, "exactly what it sounds like." I closed the door, turned on my heel, and walked back to my car.

The rest of the day was a bit of blur. I made all my deliveries and even had time to do half of Tara's. At the end of the day, Theo, Tara, and I ate dinner at Seven Sweets. After Deidra closed shop, she made a butternut squash soup for the four of us. You could tell she was exhausted. The extra business was wonderful, in a way, but it was taking a toll on her physically. You would never know this when tasting her cooking. The soup was rich and creamy, with just the right amount of spices. She paired the soup with thick pieces of buttery garlic bread. More comfort food.

The days were getting shorter and shorter. By the time dinner was served, it was already dark. Seven Sweets was our own little haven. It was our cozy little clubhouse, decorated now with so much Halloween themed décor that it could have been a craft shop. It didn't hurt that there was also an endless supply of cinnamon pumpkin cupcakes and macadamia nut white chocolate cookies. Despite our collective fatigue, we laughed and ate and laughed some more. VanHoy did not come up. It was almost as if we all sensed that we needed a break from him and the events of the last couple of days. By the end of dinner, it was almost impossible to stay awake.

Both Tara and I left our cars at The Alchemist, and Theo drove us home. On the way, we rolled down our windows and enjoyed the smell of fall all around us. I dozed in and out on the way, jolting awake with every familiar bump. *This is what it was like to drive home from the shop after a long day as a kid*, I thought hazily. Finally, I was able to make it upstairs to my large bed, covered with soft bedding and more blankets and pillows than any one person could need. I showered quickly, then I sank into the softness. There would be no reading to unwind tonight. I knew I would be out within minutes. Tomorrow, I would think of who to speak with next. Perhaps, I would make a trip over to The Witches Brew to talk with Hansen Mills. As I drifted to sleep, I wondered about the smell in Harrison's car and whether he actually drank that cup of coffee.

Chapter 5

For the first time in the last few days, I woke up well rested. I even woke up early. I silently crept through Culpepper Manor, wondering how many quiet footsteps had come before me. I had heard tell of townspeople knocking in the middle of the night when a child had been missing or when a lover had not come home. A Culpepper would know what to do. A Culpepper would be safer to talk to under the dense, heavy blanket of night. Townspersons could come in, sit nervously, confess their problems, and then scurry home on foot with a remedy. Better not bring a horse; horses draw attention. The next day, no acknowledgement of the meeting would be made, should the same person have passed a Culpepper on the street.

Occasionally, even now, these townspeople would show up at The Alchemist, although the problems seemed much smaller—a family member suffering from a cold, a child that is too dependent on technology, a lover no longer texting back. Now, friendly acknowledgements occurred on the street.

Now, remedies had changed to become 'more fun,' but the old remedies were far from forgotten. The only difference was the old remedies were no longer shared.

I reached the kitchen and decided to make myself a steaming cup of hot cocoa with peppermint. I fired up my laptop, as I was waiting for the sweet liquid to cool. I pulled up a search engine and typed in the name that had been on my mind: Hansen Mills. There was barely any information online about this fellow. The search results indicated that he had graduated high school in 1990 from a town in Georgia. He had worked for a trucking company. I sat back and wondered if this could be the same Hansen Mills. Surely, this name had to be common. I tried to think if I remembered the name Hansen Mills from growing up. Although he was much older than me, I was sure I would have heard of him if he had been from here. My mother knew basically every business owner in town. Although Mills' bar, The Witches Brew, was relatively new, the building itself was much older. It was likely that the bar opened after my mother was gone.

I typed in The Witches Brew. Surprisingly, the bar had a website, although the website was quite plain. The Witches Brew was written near the top in dripping slime-green letters. Underneath the letters was written "Cheers, Witches!" I rolled my eyes. *Tacky*. I searched the website for any information about the owner. There was a small section near the bottom with a picture of Hansen T. Mills and an acknowledgement of ownership. I quickly opened another search and typed in Hansen T. Mills' name.

After going through a couple of pages, I found some address records. According to the records, Hansen T. Mills owned a historic property in Boston, valued at over two million dollars. He owned another property in Seven Hills valued at $200,000, and another property off the coast of Massachusetts. This property was also valued at over two million dollars. My jaw dropped! *How in the world did Hansen Mills have so much money? Why would someone with that kind of money run a seedy bar in Seven Hills?*

I scrolled through a couple of other pages to try to read about his other business ventures. I found that he part-owned a junkyard business outside of Seven Hills. *How did Mills have almost five million dollars in property, while working and running The Witches Brew and a junkyard? Could these businesses be that lucrative?* I clicked on the link for the junkyard website, trying to find the name of the other partner. No information. I found the LLC information, but no other name was listed on the online paperwork.

Theo and Tara shuffled into the kitchen, both looking exhausted. I promptly made them each a cup of the peppermint hot cocoa. The scent of rich, dark chocolate and bitingly spicy peppermint filled the kitchen, comforting all of us, no doubt reminding us of many mornings before this one, sitting with our mother and our aunt, all cozy and safe. We all loved Autumn. If my mother and aunt were here, every room would have been decorated to the hilt with black cats, fat orange-and-white pumpkins, and twinkling lights. I looked around, thinking that the kitchen looked almost plain, despite the dried herbs hanging throughout the room. I made a mental note that, next year, I would decorate the whole house.

"Why are you awake so early?" Tara asked, ripping me from my thoughts. "Why are all of us up so early? We got most of the deliveries done. Now, we can go back to regular hours."

"It's not that early," Theo retorted, looking at the laptop over my shoulder and blowing into her ceramic mug. "What are you working on?"

"Remember when I told you both about the conversation Deidra and I had at Seven Sweets with Ronnie Jackman? He told us that Hansen Mills, the owner of The Witches Brew, would frequently come in unannounced to talk to VanHoy. Just now, I was poking around online and found out that he owns almost five million dollars' worth of real estate in Massachusetts. He also owns another business here. He owns a junkyard just outside of Seven Hills."

"Are you serious?" Theo asked, "Wow."

"I've been in The Witches Brew a couple of times and that place is a dump. He cannot be profiting that much from owning it. We all know that Seven Hills is not much of a party town," Tara stated, matter-of-factly. "Even during this time of the year. It gets even worse once the tourists leave."

"Of course, it is possible that his junkyard is quite lucrative," Theo stated between sips. "Who is the other owner?"

"I don't know. I have been trying to find that out myself. I think that we should wrangle up Deidra today and all go out to The Witches Brew. Let's talk to some of his staff or maybe even him if he's there. We can try to find out who the other owner is and who frequents the place," I suggested, feeling a little silly. "I mean, it couldn't hurt, right?"

"I think it sounds great!" Tara said, sounding almost enthusiastic. "We can all get dressed up and do something fun. *For once.* Maybe, we will each find a man! Or maybe we will all get murdered! Either way, it is way more exciting than what we normally do." Tara paused and then started speaking again, "Mills has five million dollars' worth of property? Maybe, I'll date 'em."

I typed in The Witches Brew address, clicked on the website, and scrolled to the picture of Mills. I turned my computer around to Tara, who was busy making herself some toast from the homemade pumpernickel bread that Deidra had made. She set down the brown and white whirls of goodness, squinted her eyes, stepped closer, and looked at the screen. The picture on the website was just a head shot of Mills. He was looking stone-faced into the camera. He had red-brown hair, and his bloated cheeks were dusted with freckles. He looked like Ronnie had described him, a walking hangover. *Who chooses this photograph for their website?* I wondered incredulously.

"Eh, maybe, I won't date him," she said, still looking at the picture. We all laughed.

We all ate breakfast leisurely, talking, laughing, and playing on our phones. Since we did not have to be at the store until normal opening time, probably only one person really had to be there. We were all caught up on orders, and most of the deliveries had been made. Further, all our customers were happy with their deliveries so far. Now, we were able to sort of sit back and relax until the Christmas season began. Almost immediately following Thanksgiving, the madness would begin again. People would rush in for homemade creams, salves, ornaments, herbs, books, and, hopefully this year, homemade candles to give as gifts or stocking stuffers. Not to mention, for the last three years, we had been fulfilling online orders.

"The Witches Brew doesn't even open until 3 pm," I said, scrolling through the website yet again. "After work, we can come home, get ready, and eat a late dinner at 7:30. I'll text Deidra and ask her if she wants to come out with us."

"That sounds good," Theo nodded.

"Should I invite Ronnie?" I asked, the thought coming to me suddenly. We all looked at each other.

"Is Ronnie, like, part of the gang now?" Tara asked teasingly.

"He is. He's sort-of part of our crime-solving group," Theo said with a laugh. "Maybe we should invite him."

"I will text him and tell him to meet us there," I said decidedly.

Tara and Theo left the kitchen. Theo probably went upstairs to get ready for a long day of work. Tara probably went back upstairs to go to sleep. She would come into The Alchemist later. At this point in our lives, we all knew each other's schedules and routines. Once I was alone, I reopened the search engine and typed in Detective Harrison's full name. The computer began to 'think.' I looked around again. *Why did I feel like I was doing something wrong?* Given the circumstances, it would be perfectly reasonable that I would Google him. Many pages popped up.

I clicked on the first story, entitled "Boston Detective Shot During Raid: Detective Involved in Opioid Drug Ring." I quickly skimmed through the article, my heart rate picking up. The article, written by a local Boston journalist, first discussed the opioid epidemic nationally, then homed in on it in Massachusetts, particularly in Boston. According to the author, Boston law-enforcement officers were tracking a group of drug dealers thought to be responsible for selling opioids to many locals, including minors. The lead detectives on the case were Detective Harrison and his partner, Detective Joel Miller.

One night, the detectives were led to a home thought to be a meeting site for the dealers. During the home raid, Detective Miller shot Detective Harrison in the side, narrowly missing his heart. Harrison survived by running into the basement, locking the door, and then breaking and crawling out of a window. The heavy locks on the inside of the basement door were thought to have saved his life. There was evidence in the home that Miller and others were attempting to break down the heavy, wooden door secured by two dead bolt locks. By the time Harrison had crawled out of the tiny window, backup had arrived. After the incident and months of FBI investigation, there was evidence uncovered that revealed that Detective Miller had been in cahoots with the local dealers.

Over the course of a year, Detective Miller was thought to have accepted over $80,000 of bribery money in exchange for providing information to known offenders, Jonathan McCready and Nathaniel Mathers, who were also in the home at the time of the shooting. After a year of investigation, McCready and Mathers were brought up on a series of charges. Both were set to face charges in the spring of this year. Detective Miller, however, was never brought up on any charges; he shot himself inside his home, before law enforcement could enter and arrest him. Detectives Harrison and Miller had been partners for five years prior to the incident.

I blinked at my computer, stunned. I could still feel my heart beating through my chest. I began to click on other stories, looking for more information. Many articles told the same or a similar story. One article discussed Detective Miller's wife and children, all of whom had moved from Massachusetts, not long after the scandal. I looked at the picture of Detective Miller on one article entitled, "Disgraced Detective Suicides After Drug Raid." He was a tall, blonde, handsome, all-American looking guy. He looked like the boy-next-door, all-grown-up. There was another picture of him with Detective Harrison. The two looked like a picture out of a calendar that you might pick up as a gag-gift entitled, 'Sexy Detectives.' But, of course, the pair were dressed in suits instead of bare-chested.

Detective Harrison was handsome with black hair and piercing light eyes. The picture was in black and white, but I knew from real life that his eyes were a crystal blue. There was just a bit of stubble on his face. If Detective Miller was an all-American boy, then Harrison was the quintessential bad-boy. I closed my eyes and remembered him sitting next to me in his car; he was striking. It was no wonder that, according to local gossip, he had many, many conquests. His charms went unnoticed the first time I met him. Of course, there were the circumstances under which we met. Not to mention, he had a consistent sardonic manner, which made him less tolerable than he might have been under other circumstances. I closed my laptop, trying to process the information that I had just learned. I breathed deeply, remembering the smell of mahogany in his car.

The Alchemist was surprisingly busy. Theo had to call both Tara and me in early to help with the influx of customers and orders made that day. The day went by in a blur. By the time closing rolled around, we were all tired and ready to go. We raced home in our respective vehicles to get ready for our planned night out.

I stood in my bathroom, feeling a little anxious and excited. It had been a while since I had the chance to get all dressed up and go out. Of course, I had been out a few times, dabbled on some dating sites, and had a few dinners paid for by prospective suitors. Most of the experiences had been awkward, dull, and only vaguely memorable. Most of the men I met on the sites were much older than their pictures, looked different from their pictures, seemed to be interested in going out on as many dates as possible, were out-of-towners looking for brief fun, or worse—someone who was 'interested' in my family.

I met a gentleman, if you could call him that, on a dating website last year. He was tall, good-looking, and lived just 20 minutes outside of Seven Hills. We texted back and forth through the website app quite a bit before we decided to meet. I liked that he was a bit older than I was, probably around 15 years older. He seemed established, different from the men my age in Seven Hills or others on the app. We met at a restaurant just outside of Seven Hills. Two rich, buttery, pasta dishes and a bottle of red wine later, we were seated on the same side of the table, laughing over anything and everything. *He is even more handsome than his pictures*, I thought while his face was so close to mine, his hand on my thigh.

"I have to confess something," he said, as the laughter started to die down.

"Oh, yeah?" I said, hoping it would not be that he had a wife and children waiting for him at home.

"I've heard of you before. I remember the news coverage of when your father went missing," he said quietly.

He did not look me. I did not look at him. I was happy I was not sitting across from him. I felt as if someone had slapped me across the face, every muscle in my body turning into stone, my emotions blurred by red wine. My head buzzed. Both of us were silent for so long that, for a second, I thought that I had imagined the whole thing.

"What?" I stammered, finally breaking the silence.

"I didn't realize it at first, but I recognized your name from the news coverage. Treasure is not a name you hear very often," he responded.

I said nothing.

"I'm sorry," he said, looking down at the table. "I should not have brought that up."

"Excuse me," I said, rising, and grabbing my purse.

I pretended to walk towards the restroom, but instead, I walked right out of the exit. I felt sick. Under any other circumstances, I probably would have stuck it out. However, the alcohol was making me braver than usual. After leaving the restaurant, I walked a couple of blocks, called Deidra, and she picked me up.

"What happened?" she asked, as I entered her car. Her car always seemed to smell like powdered sugar and baking spices.

I sighed, "A waste of my time happened."

She nodded. She just accepted this answer and did not press me for details. She turned up the radio, and we drove home singing 90s songs at the top of our lungs. I hung my arm out of the window and felt the cool wind rush through my fingers. A heavy blanket of anxiety rested on my body. *"I've heard of you before. I remember the news coverage of when your father went missing,"* replayed in my brain.

When I got home, I ran upstairs and flung myself onto my big comfy bed. I shoved my head into a cool, white pillow, the smell of detergent and bleach filling my nostrils. Theo always used so much bleach. The word sterile popped into my head. I liked the idea of my life becoming sterile. *Bleached.* The red wine had finally worn off a bit, replaced by a dull headache from the sweet liquid and the loud music in the car. I opened the dating app one last time to find a message that just read, "I'm sorry."

"Let's get wild!" Tara said, coming down the stairs. She was wearing a black cocktail dress that left little to the imagination.

"You know we're going to The Witches Brew, right?" I asked, looking at her and shaking my head. She looked ridiculous.

"I do," she responded. "Why are you dressed like Tim Allen from *Home Improvement*?"

"Funny," I said, looking down at my flannel and jeans. I had dressed up a bit, adding some gold bracelets and cute, fall booties.

"Let's get going, ladies!" Theo said, the constant director. "Don't forget that we aren't going to get wild. We are going to find out a little information about Mills."

"I'm sure we can do both," Tara said. "You are always telling me to multitask, Theo."

Deidra laughed, "Ah, sisters…I'm glad I'm an only child."

I nudged her with my hip. "You're the fourth Culpepper."

The Witches Brew was exactly how I imagined it. It was dark, dank, and at the moment, only sparsely populated. The four of us piled into a large, corner booth, under a neon sign that read: Drink. Drank. Drunk. *Clever*, I thought with a sigh. The table was, of course, sticky.

"Are we almost done?" I asked, pulling my fingers from the table.

"This was *your* idea," Deidra reminded, pulling some disinfectant wipes out of her purse. She tossed the travel sized packet at me from across the table.

"Hello, ladies," a man's voice said. "Mind if I sit down?"

We all looked over to see Ronnie.

"Hi, Ronnie!" Theo exclaimed. "Of course! How are you doing?!" Theo seemed so excited to see him that I thought she might throw her arms around him. God, she was so friendly. Just like Mom.

"I'm good. I'm really good," he responded. "Ready for our night out!"

"What are you working on right now?" Theo asked, "I'm a *huge* fan of your work."

"Well, right now, I'm working on compiling an oral history of Seven—"

Before Ronnie could finish, Tara interrupted, "I'm going to sit at the bar!" She scooted out of the seat and started walking over to the bar.

"I'm so sorry," Theo said, looking horrified at Ronnie.

"We think she might have an asshole-disorder," I said, with a smile.

"No. No. No," Ronnie said, with a laugh. "It's okay. Let's not talk about work."

"Let's get a little food, a couple drinks, and make a game-plan for what we want to find out," Deidra said, conspiratorially. "Let's see if we can find out who frequents the bar. We want to know who Mills' partner is. Maybe, he has an office in the back like I do at Seven Sweets. Perhaps, some of the staff have even seen VanHoy here. Maybe they've heard things. I know a lot of my staff probably overhear my conversations with all of you. I'm sure they know more about me—about us—than I think they do."

"Good point. But how should we go about bringing all of this up?" asked Theo. "Maybe we should desert the booth and head to the bar? Go make conversation with the bartenders?"

"Good idea," Ronnie chimed in. "Besides, this table is sticky."

We all joined Tara at the bar. She already had a drink in hand, seemingly bought for her by the older gentleman chatting with her on the barstool next to her. He looked quite a bit older than Tara, perhaps in his late forties. He had silver-brown hair, a farmer's tan, and a shiny, gold wedding ring that he twisted around his finger nervously. He had no reason to be nervous or hopeful. Tara had no real interest in him.

"Can I buy you a drink?" Ronnie asked, sitting on a barstool next to me. "Or is coffee and doughnuts more appropriate for a stake-out?"

"I'll take a drink," I said, with a smile.

Tara was right. This was more fun than what we normally did on Friday nights, which was basically stay at home and read or binge-watch Netflix.

"Maybe just a beer? I don't know if I would trust their mixed drinks, or their coffee and doughnuts, for that matter."

"Yes, I think a beer is probably a safe bet," he said, nodding at the bartender and placing an order.

The bartender was a plump, blonde woman. She looked young, probably Tara's age. A deep part showed off that her hair was shaved on one side. This was in stark contrast to the ringlets of bleached curls that hung to her other shoulder. Both shoulders were littered with tattoos. The one touched by the curls displayed an Alice and Wonderland themed sleeve. The other hosted a gang of skeletons decked out in ballgowns.

"Hi, Dr. Jackman," she said, looking squarely at Ronnie.

"Oh my gosh, hi! How are you? Alexis, right?" He responded.

"Yes, you remembered!" She said with a laugh, looking at him brightly.

We all stared at each other for a moment.

"Forgive me, Alexis. This is my friend, Treasure," he said, making a gesture towards me. "Alexis was one of my students–"

"I was in his Oral Histories of Seven Hills class," she said proudly. "I loved that class."

He smiled warmly, "when do you graduate?"

"Next spring," she said with a smile. I can't wait to get out into the workforce. "I am a criminal justice major. I want to be like one of those people on *Criminal Minds* or *Law and Order*. You know, going after the bad guy. I took your class for fun."

"Ah, nice," he said nodding.

Suddenly, I saw an in. I asked this in a light, friendly tone. "How do you like working here? Do you know Hansen Mills well?"

"It's ok," she said with a smile. "It's a job." She did not say anything about Mills.

"Well Treasure and I...we're actually...we're actually working on a project together. We are working on an article about The All Hallows' Eve

Pageant and Mayor VanHoy's involvement, as a way to, you know, honor his memory."

"Yes, that is horrible what happened," she said with a sigh. "Too bad I'm not on the job yet. I could solve the crime!"

Ronnie and I looked at each other and laughed nervously.

"Did you ever meet Mayor VanHoy?" I asked.

"I never met him, even though, you know, he would stop in from time to time," she said causally.

"Really?" Ronnie and I said, in unison.

She laughed, "Yes, well...I think he owns part of this bar. I think Hansen had mentioned that before. Of course, he says a lot of things." She lowered her voice, "he's drunk...a lot."

We both nodded. "Does Mills have an office here?" I asked, then added, "we would love to ask him—talk with him—about VanHoy, given that they were...friendly."

Ronnie nodded, chiming in, "great idea, Treasure. A personal touch. I love it."

The phrase, *I love it,* seemed wildly out of place coming out of Ronnie's mouth. We were not only trying to 'solve' a murder because of Culpepper paranoia and Deidra's business reputation, but now we were involved in some horrible community theatre act-out. Next, I would slap Ronnie across the face and faint from the *overwhelmingness of it all*. I had to laugh. I suddenly felt ridiculous. *Were we all playing with fire?* Surely, we all didn't believe that unrelated incidents years apart would cast suspicion on our family. Perhaps, instead of ordering beers in a bar, we all needed to sit in a therapist's chair.

However, everyone's spirits seemed high. Tara was having more fun than ever. Deidra and Theo were laughing a few seats down, talking to Brent Silverton, a man with whom we all went to high school. Even I was having a good time, enjoying Ronnie's company. Maybe this was where we needed to be right now.

"I love it too," was all I said.

"Yea, he has an office in the back. He's not in yet. I am sure he'll be in later though. Two beers?" Alexis asked.

"Yes," we said, again in unison.

One beer turned to two beers, which turned into four beers, which quickly turned into six. The beers were multiplying. My head was buzzing. Out of nowhere, The Witches Brew had become crowded. *Perhaps, this is a profitable business*, I thought. At around 10 pm, tables were moved out of the way to create a make-shift dance floor. Tara was on the floor with the nameless, older man with the wedding ring. Some sort of country-pop mix blasted through the speakers. Deidra, Theo, and Brent were now standing by the bar. I noticed that they had ordered a round— or two—of shots and the empty glasses sat on a tray beside them. So much for, *we aren't getting wild*. We were all going to need a ride home.

Even Ronnie seemed to have had more drinks than were usual for him. He talked with several students and other patrons of The Witches Brew. His students seemed to love him. I was surprised at how many we ran into here, although I shouldn't have been. It was a bar, even if it was The Witches Brew. Many patrons, particularly the older male patrons, were excited to see him, to ask him questions, and to buy him a drink. A local celebrity at a bar. When I was with Ronnie, it was sometimes difficult to remember that he was pseudo-famous. Hanging out at The Witches Brew was a reminder.

Ronnie was talking to yet another 'fan' of his work, when I noticed a head of dark, glossy hair through the crowd. The man was fit, tall, and broad shouldered. By someone more impressed than me, he could be described as a 'tall drink of water.' He wore grey pants with a light blue collared shirt. His shirt was tucked in. My eyes burned into the back of his skull because, of course, I knew who he was. Detective Harrison. Ronnie kept talking, Deidra and Theo kept laughing, and Tara kept dancing, all unaware that a shark had entered the water. *What was he doing here?* I wondered. *Was he here for fun? Did he have the same suspicions about Mills?* I walked over to Deidra, Theo, and Brent. I took an untouched shot that was sitting on the counter. It was warm and burned all the way down. I was going to be hungover tomorrow.

"Harrison is here," I said calmly.

Theo looked alarmed, "What? Where?"

I pointed to him, trying to be causal and inconspicuous. Deidra looked behind her.

"Why do you think he's here?" she asked.

"I don't know," I answered, although I could think of a few reasons. He's following us. He suspects us or Deidra. Maybe he suspects Mills? Or he simply wanted to go out. Surely, detectives went out for drinks. Besides, we never go here. How would he know he could find us here?

Theo returned as the voice of reason, although I noticed her speech was a bit slurred, "Oh well, we're not doing anything wrong. We are just out, having some fun."

Brent, who still stood with us, looked confused. "What did I miss?" He asked, good naturedly.

"Oh, nothing," said Deidra unconvincingly.

Brent shrugged, disinterested, and sipped from his beer. Just then, someone grabbed Brent from behind, lifting him up. The beer he was sipping ran down his chin and onto his shirt.

"What the…," Brent said, turning around to see Cliff Bishop. "Cliff!" Brent exclaimed. "Now, it's a party!"

Cliff laughed and motioned for the bartender, Alexis, to come over. Despite Cliff spending years at a desk, away from the football field, he was still incredibly large and muscular.

"How's it going Cliff?" Brent asked. "Here alone tonight?"

"Who would I be with?" Cliff asked and laughed.

I noticed Harrison moving towards a high-top table with a gorgeous, young blonde. This was one possibility I hadn't thought of earlier: he was on a date. I suddenly felt sick and drunk. Very drunk. That last shot must have pushed me over the edge. Without saying a word, I moved away from Deidra, Theo, Cliff, and Brent. I made a beeline for the bathroom, which was on the other end of the bar, closer to Harrison; lights and faces blurred as I passed. I hoped I would make it to the bathroom. The hallway to the bathroom seemed exceptionally long and dark. I had the sensation that I was walking through a tunnel. I saw the ladies and the gentlemen signs down the hall to the left. I stopped on my way in front of a door that read "Office." For a moment, I debated walking in. I would have the perfect excuse. I'm drunk. On the other hand, I did not know what I was looking for or what was I hoping to find. Where would I even begin to look? What if Mills was in there? I kept walking.

The bathroom was as gross as expected, but everything seemed dulled right now, and I didn't care. I waited my turn, walked into a stall, and vomited up the warm shot I took earlier. The smell of sick and alcohol filled the stall. I tried not to look at the toilet. If I did, I would vomit again. I flushed and walked out. A woman behind me looked at me, disgusted. I hoped she wasn't one of Ronnie's students. I looked in the mirror and tried to fix up my face. I used a wet edge of a paper towel to wipe some of the smudged mascara from under my eyes. I dug into my small clutch for some sort of makeup and half-heartedly tried to fix my face. I wish I had mouthwash. I still felt drunk, but I felt much better.

I stumbled out of the bathroom and passed a man while going down the long, tunnel hall. The man lightly touched my arm as I tried to pass. I jumped back as if the man had injured me. I whipped my head back to look at him. The man was Detective Harrison.

"Treasure," Harrison said softly, even kindly. His voice was like silk coated with honey. "You alright?"

I felt embarrassed seeing him in my drunken state. He looked so handsome. I wanted to put my hands on his arms to steady myself. I felt like that could help.

"Detective Harrison," I said, trying to make my voice sound even. "How are you?"

He laughed, "Not as good as you." His eyes glittered in the darkness. He was making fun of me.

I rolled my eyes. "What are you doing here?"

"I'm out with a friend," he said, then grinned.

"Yes, she looks like a great friend. Were you two in the same fraternity or something?" I asked, matching his mocking tone.

"So, you noticed me?" He said, in a mock-flirty tone. He laughed softly. "I was never in a fraternity. Speaking of academia, I see you are here with Dr. Jackman. How is your project coming? You know the article about VanHoy—I mean the All Hallows' Eve Pageant." He had obviously made the mistake on purpose. *Were we all this transparent?*

I opened my mouth to respond, but he cut me off, "it has to be hard to get work done here. It's so loud." He pointed into the air to reference the country-pop music that was still blaring.

"Shouldn't you be working?" I asked, and my tone sounded more accusatory than I intended. "A man was murdered."

"I'm always working," he reassured me, his tone serious. "You and your family should have more faith in law enforcement."

I snorted, "what does that mean? We're not the Manson family for pity's sake!"

He threw his head back and laughed. He smelled so good, and I felt so out of control. I felt the urge to put my hands on his forearms again. I wanted to sit down.

"Treasure!" Deidra yelled over the music. She was practically jogging down the hall.

She looked stunned as she came closer. "Detective Harrison? What are *you* doing here? Are you following us? I can't dare to think that you would question us in a bar of all places!"

He paused, looking exasperated, "I'm not questioning anyone. And yes, I can ask questions anywhere I go. You can't walk into a bar and yell 'Sanctuary!' and think that I can't come in."

"He wasn't questioning me," I said softly.

"I was checking on her," Harrison stated, matter-of-factly.

Deidra looked from me to Harrison and back to me. She nodded. "Ok. Well, Treasure, we are all ready to leave."

"Say hi to your *friend* for me," I said to Harrison, moving past them to begin the walk down the hall.

He laughed, "we aren't that good of friends, Treasure. You and I are *much* better friends."

I let out a snort, "we are *not* friends."

He looked at me and grinned, "we have had a conversation outside of work at least twice. That basically makes you my best friend in town."

I laughed, took a step back, grabbed Deidra, linked my arm in hers, and began walking down the hall. I was so thankful I had Deidra to escort me. Surely, I would not be able to walk even a semi-straight line without her.

Tara, Theo, and Ronnie were already waiting for us when we reached the front door of the bar. The older gentleman with the wedding ring was also lurking nearby. I had a feeling after a night of dancing with Tara, he was not quite ready to say goodbye. Perhaps, he believed she would change her mind at the last minute. I knew she wouldn't. Ronnie, Theo, Tara, Deidra, and I said our goodbyes and thanked each other for a fun night. We all vowed to do it again sometime. After a few minutes, Theo, Tara, and I hopped into an Uber that Theo had ordered for us. Ronnie and Deidra were left behind, waiting for their respective cars. I leaned my elbow on the side of the car, staring out of the window. My phone buzzed in my clutch. I unlocked my phone to a text from Deidra that read, "What in the actual fuck was that?"

Chapter 6

As I woke the next morning, the lingering effects of too much alcohol could still be felt in my stomach and head. Not too bad, getting sick at the bar probably had helped, but I still felt gross. Not that I knew for certain, but I believed that my breath must be something on the order of dead dog. *Ugh.* I looked down at my phone and saw that Theo had already left for the store and evidently had the good sense not to try to wake Tara or me. She probably bounced out of bed this morning, just like any other, with a flock of little mice and birdies to help her dress. I continued to lie in bed and stared at the ceiling. Last night had been fun, but we definitely did not get as much information out of our evening as I had hoped. Talking with the young bartender Alexis had helped. At least we now knew VanHoy did have a business relationship with Mills. And the employees considered him to be a boss or owner. That was something, I guess. I wondered if it really mattered.

I finally mustered the energy to extricate myself from the bed and hit the shower. Not long after, I slowly made my way to town and Seven Sweets. I smiled when I saw Deidra, who was looking a little haggard. She joined me at the rear booth with two coffee cups and a carafe.

"A single cup didn't even seem worth it," she said sitting down. She poured us both a cup, and we sipped in silence for a moment.

"So, how are you?" I said with a slight giggle.

"Well," she sighed, "Decent, but I have a pounding headache."

"I know," I said, shaking my head. "We can't hang."

"So," Deidra started, her voice fallen into a serious tone, "Detective Harrison? What's going on?"

I shrugged.

"Treasure," she pressed. "I'm serious. What was that last night? Was he trying to question you?"

"I'm sorry.... I'm not trying to be evasive." I paused, trying to find the right words. "I don't think he was following us or trying to interrogate me. He had no way to know that we'd be there, and he was with a date. But he was asking questions. I don't know...part of me thinks he was trying to be...friendly...?" My voice went up higher at the end. *I sounded like a teenager.*

"Friendly?" Deidra said, raising her eyebrows. "Treasure..."

"I know, I know," I cut her off. "I really don't know what that was. I wasn't in the best frame of mind."

Deidra nodded.

"No, you weren't. That's why I went over to you."

She took a slow sip of her coffee then stared at me for a moment. I knew Deidra long enough to know that she was about to say something really serious. I braced myself.

"Treasure, do you like him?"

"No," I responded immediately, with a surprising amount of confidence. "I don't like him. Plus, you know how I feel about...um...law enforcement. I think I could have like PTSD or something."

"I think you probably do," she said softly, compassionately. She then shifted her tone. She sounded more causal when she asked, "Do you think he likes you?"

Her question gave me some butterflies in my stomach, which I quickly dismissed as the lingering effects of the party flu.

"I don't think so." I took a giant gulp of coffee. "My overwhelming concern during every interaction with Harrison is that one of us is going to end up in handcuffs. I mean, I think he comes across as professional, right? More professional than other cops we've dealt with in the past? When he's not, you know, *being him*, I guess."

Deidra nodded in agreement.

"I'm waiting for him to yell, 'Gotcha!' because of something I've said during one of these seemingly casual interactions."

As I said that, I realized that it would be nice to actually trust someone outside of the family and Deidra, to trust law enforcement to do their job without bias. Maybe that was Harrison, but at the moment, I wasn't sure, and it would be better to err on the side of caution. Deidra smiled, which warmed my heart.

"I'm here for you," she reminded me. "Always have been, always will. I'm totally Team Culpepper."

We both laughed, which quickly turned into dueling groans as we reached for our aching heads.

Tara joined Theo and me at the store at her regular time, sunglasses on, with a mere grunt acknowledgment, in true Tara fashion. She barely stood up for a full hour after she arrived, rolling her eyes when a customer suggested that she help her. *Maybe Theo will actually kill her*, I thought to myself and smiled. There wasn't much talk at work today. Even our bickering slowed to a snail's pace. This gave me time to think about VanHoy, Mills, Harrison, and occasionally even Harrison's arms in the hallway. Last night gave me more questions. I wanted to do something, but I was not sure exactly what that something was.

Around 4 o'clock, Theo was busy with a customer, so I decided it would be a good time to leave with minimal questions. I quickly walked to the back to grab my bag and coat.

"Where are you going?" I practically jumped out of my skin, Tara startling me from behind.

"I have an idea, but I don't want to tell you about it."

"Why not?" she said stepping closer.

"Plausible deniability."

"Cool," Tara said, turning on her heals to leave the room. "I'll see you later tonight. Call me if you need to be bailed out."

I paused, thinking about what she said. *No*, I said, shaking my head, *focus*. I left The Alchemist and headed towards town hall, hoping Ronnie was still working. I got excited when I saw his car in the parking lot. After parking in the far back corner, I jogged towards the building, quickly jumping up the front stairs. Ronnie's office was the first one on the left. I wondered briefly what it would be like to have an office, a *real* job. As I got to the door, I stopped for a second to catch my breath and to still my heart. *I really do need to get back to the gym*. I knocked on the door and heard a chair move on the inside.

"Treasure?!" Ronnie said after pulling open the door. He looked surprised but elated. "I wasn't expecting to see you. Please," he said gesturing to the chairs inside, "come in and grab a seat."

"I'm sorry to just show up unannounced," I said falling into a chair in front of his desk. "I hope I'm not interrupting."

"Not at all," he said smiling. "I could use a break. My head is a little foggy today." We both chuckled.

"Speaking of foggy heads," I said giggling, "you're like a celebrity." Ronnie blushed.

"No, no," he said shaking his hands. "Everyone just knows everyone else 'round here. You know what it's like."

"Um, I don't think anyone was nearly as excited to see anyone else in that bar last night." Ronnie shook his head.

"Oh, come on. Everyone gets excited to see you too. Speaking of, um, so I have to ask," Ronnie said, concern appearing on his face. "What's up with you and Detective Harrison? Are you two...."

"No," I stated firmly, for the second time in a day. "I don't know what that was."

"Okay," Ronnie slowly continued, "was he trying to question you?"

"Well, no," I stammered, "I mean, he knows that we aren't working on an article, and he's sort of just like, um, mocking me over it."

"Oh," Ronnie said, his eyes going wide. "Really?"

"Yeah, so...I just don't know what to do with that. My sisters and I were already on his radar. And now he obviously knows we are looking into things on our own. He's annoyed by it, but sometimes I think he finds it amusing." I shrugged.

"Huh," Ronnie said rubbing his chin. "Okay, but there's nothing personal?"

"Ronnie," I felt myself starting to get flustered. Again, I felt annoyed but slightly charged up, my body coming alive. I took in a breath to steady myself. "I don't trust him. I really don't know what to make of these seemingly *'friendly'*..." I paused to emphasize the word, putting it in air quotes, "interactions. I'm truly concerned about what's going to happen to me and my sisters."

Ronnie nodded.

"I'm sorry," Ronnie said, reaching across the table. He did not grab my hand; instead, he put his next to mine. "This must be really distressing for you all."

I swallowed hard. It was. *When would it get easier?* The thought made me sick to my stomach or, at least, sicker to my stomach.

"Anyway," I said, changing the subject, "can we talk about the bartender Alexis? Your former student? I was thinking more about what she said about VanHoy. That's interesting, right? We already knew VanHoy and Mills had a lot of interactions here, but it was interesting to find out there was some interaction concerning the bar."

"Definitely," Ronnie agreed, his tone becoming more serious. "They were working together on something. Now, we just need to figure out exactly what that was. I did do some checking on the bar ownership," Ronnie said, pulling a file from his lower desk drawer. "There is a share of ownership that belongs to someone else, but it's not listed as a person. It's Wicking LLC," he said, turning the papers so I could read them.

I quickly scanned the documents.

"This confirms what I found on an internet search yesterday, that an LLC is a partial owner. Alexis mentioned that Mills said VanHoy owned part of the bar. Do you think VanHoy is Wicking LLC?"

"Maybe," Ronnie said. "I haven't found anything else that ties VanHoy to Wicking, but that could be the connection. That would explain why Mills was always over here with VanHoy. Maybe they were just business partners."

"Absolutely—makes sense. Why be all secretive about it then?" I asked, half rhetorically.

"Well, VanHoy was an elected official. Maybe he didn't want to be associated with a grungy bar."

"But he already had a shady reputation," I countered. "At that point, why would owning a bar matter? Maybe he would have lost some votes, but he always wins by a landslide."

"True," Ronnie acknowledged. "So, let's spend some time tracking down more information on this Wicking LLC. At least we'll know if it's associated with VanHoy. If not, then VanHoy and Mills had some other dealings."

"Okay," I said, sliding forward in my chair. "There is a second reason why I wanted to come and see you today."

"Oh," Ronnie said, leaning forward as well. "I can't wait!"

"I haven't said this to anyone else, but it would be really useful to look through some of VanHoy's papers to see if anything links them together."

"Well, right," Ronnie said nodding, "but how are we going to do that? You want to go ask Mrs. VanHoy to look through her husband's papers?"

"No," I said, looking at Ronnie squarely in the eye, "I don't want to ask anyone. I want to go down the hall and look through VanHoy's filing cabinets."

It took a moment, but recognition slowly appeared on Ronnie's face.

"Um, Treasure…"

"Hear me out," I interrupted, holding up my hand. "I don't get a sense that the police are sniffing around Mills at all. Do you think they know Mills had been meeting here with VanHoy?"

"Well, probably not," Ronnie said, rubbing his chin. "We know most of those meetings weren't on his calendar. I don't think even Nancy knew the extent to which they were meeting. And now that you mention it, no one from the police ever asked me anything about VanHoy, or Mills, or anything else." Ronnie looked perplexed by his last statement. "Yeah, so how *would* they know? I'm the person right by the door, and no one ever came to talk to me." Ronnie fell back into his chair.

"Exactly. So, they aren't even looking at Hansen Mills. I personally believe that a shady business partner is a prime suspect."

"Agreed," Ronnie chuckled. "I mean, I watch *CSI*."

"So," I said smiling coyly, "do you want to help me break into VanHoy's office?"

About a half an hour later, I was sitting quietly in Ronnie's office, waiting for him to return from a brief, fact-finding mission. Breaking into an office in a building, where Ronnie had permission to be, was one thing. We could probably explain away our reasons for being there if anyone caught us. However, breaking into an office that had been sealed by the police during the course of a homicide investigation was another thing entirely. Thankfully, Ronnie had remembered that VanHoy's office had been sealed by the police the morning after his murder. Officers had placed a large evidence sticker over the opening of the door that would show if someone unauthorized had entered. That was enough to make me lose my nerve. We nearly called off our plan, but then Ronnie offered to casually walk by the office to see if it was still sealed. While I waited for him to return, I started nervously picking at my fingernails. Then my mind started wandering, fantasizing that Ronnie had been caught by Harrison and was in the process of being hauled off to jail. My heart started to pound so loudly that I didn't hear the approaching footsteps. I nearly jumped out of my skin when Ronnie excitedly burst through his office door.

"It's gone!" he whispered.

I put my hands on my chest and started to breathe heavily.

"Are you okay," he asked, jumping in front of me.

"I'm fine, I'm fine," I said, mostly for myself. "You startled me, that's all." Ronnie had the biggest grin on his face, causing me to smile back.

"So now, we just wait," Ronnie said, dropping into his chair behind the desk. "By 9 pm, everyone should be out of the building."

"Okay," I said, calming down. I looked at my phone. It was 4:43 pm. *We have some serious time to kill*, I thought. Ronnie and I starred at each other for a couple of uncomfortable moments, each of us politely smiling. *Oh, this is going to be long night.* Clearly sensing the building discomfort, Ronnie cleared his throat, then opened his top desk drawer, revealing a worn deck of playing cards.

"Go Fish?" he suggested.

After multiple, surprisingly entertaining rounds of Go Fish, Ronnie again exited his office, this time to snatch us some dinner from the vending machines outside of the break room. While he was gone, I took the opportunity to stretch my legs and started snooping around his office. Ronnie was clearly very interested in the history of Seven Hills. Large city maps were stacked on a table underneath the window facing the front parking lot. Multiple town directories littered his bookshelves. On a bookshelf behind his desk, I saw several books related to the witch trials in Salem, as well as the ones in Seven Hills. Ronnie had already made our family connection to Sarah Culpepper. I was starting to wonder what else he had uncovered about our history. I moved on to other areas in the office and couldn't help but smile. Ronnie Jackman was an old soul, as my mother would have said. Having an office in a historic town hall clearly suited him.

Ronnie slowly pushed open the door to his office, smiling when he saw me.

"Okay," he said, unloading his haul on the desk, "we've got peanut butter cheese crackers that look like they've been in the vending machine since the Nixon administration."

I laughed returning to the chair in front of his desk.

"Peanut M&Ms, licorice, three granola bars, and a bag of pretzels. And to drink, I've scored us some diet Dr. Peppers. Totally awesome, right?"

"Yes, totally awesome!"

"Well, help yourself!" he said, gesturing over the pile. "We aim to please here at the Seven Hills Town Hall."

"Thank you," I said, reaching for a granola bar. I looked up at Ronnie, and giving him a sideways glance, slowly reached for the M&Ms.

"You're going to have to share those," he said flatly, barely containing another smile.

"Fine," I said with fake sarcasm, "if I must." I opened the M&Ms and put the package between us. "So," I started unwrapping my granola bar, "all-time favorite costume from the All Hallows' Eve party. Go!"

"Oh, wow," Ronnie said, pushing his chair closer to his desk. "Okay, okay...I would have to say.... Alright, I'm not just saying this because you are sitting in front of me...."

"Okay...." I laughed.

"Seriously, you and your sisters as the Sanderson Sisters from *Hocus Pocus*. That was pretty epic!"

"Really?" I laughed. "All-time favorite? Come on, Ronnie!"

"I'm serious, Treasure! Those costumes were legit. Everybody thought so!" Mom was still alive when we went as the Sanderson Sisters. I smiled at the memory. That had been a good Halloween.

"Alright, I'll let you have it," I said.

"What about you?" he asked.

"Well, actually, my sisters and I were just discussing this the other day."

"And?" he pressed.

"My favorite was you as Daniel Defoe." Ronnie nearly choked on his Dr. Pepper.

"You can't be serious?!" he said, wiping his chin.

"I am serious!" I countered. "I just thought it was so smart. Obviously, it was a precursor for what was to come…" I said, motioning around his office.

"Well, I'm honored," Ronnie said, chuckling. "I put a lot of thought into that costume."

"Well, it showed."

"So…why didn't you ever enter the pageant?" Ronnie asked tentatively. "Your mom was always so involved."

"Sarah Tarleton," I said, matter-of-factly, and we both started laughing. "Seriously," I continued, "there was no way I was competing with that!"

"Come on!" Ronnie smirked, "*she ain't all that!*"

"'*She ain't all that*'?!" I repeated back to him. For a moment I forgot that we were supposed to be hiding out and let out a loud laugh. I quickly put my hands over my mouth as Ronnie shushed me, barely containing his own laughter. "I can't believe you just said *that*" I said, wiping the tears from my eyes.

"Well, she isn't. I don't see the appeal."

"Well, you're the only one Ronnie Jackman," I said, shaking my head.

"So, she's blonde? Whatever," he said, waving his hand.

"So, you're telling me that you were the only boy in school who didn't have a crush on Sarah Tarleton?"

"I don't think I was the only one, Treasure. There was an underground movement that you clearly weren't aware of."

"Oh! Well! I stand corrected! So, who did you have a thing for in high school?"

"I'm not prepared to state that at this time," Ronnie said, raising his eyebrows as he took a sip of his Dr. Pepper. I laughed. "What about you, Treasure? Please don't tell me it was Cliff Bishop." Ronnie shook his head in disgust.

"Um, no," I replied easily, "I did not have a thing for 'The Bish.' He was terrible."

"Agreed," Ronnie said, reaching for an M&M. "I had to tutor him all though high school. I'm surprised he graduated."

"I guess I always assumed someone did his homework for him," I mused.

"Well, I can honestly say that person was not me. Probably Sarah."

"Yeah," I agreed.

We both paused when we heard voices outside of Ronnie's office door. Whatever meeting was being held on the first floor sounded like it was starting to wrap up. We heard a small group exit the front doors and walk into the parking lot.

"Ronnie, what made you come back to Seven Hills?" I asked.

"Well, I started working on my current project involving historical families in the Massachusetts settlements, and I thought I needed to get back to the source. There's just something about actually living in a place that makes it easier to write about it. There's just so much history in Seven Hills. I feel more energized here." He looked at me rather sheepishly. "That probably sounds really silly," he admitted.

"No, I get that," I countered. "There's energy here." I stopped myself short and looked in his direction. My comment didn't seem to elicit any further questioning. "How long do you plan on staying?" I continued.

"I don't know," he said, shaking his head. "I mean, I don't have any plans to leave. If I stayed here for the rest of my life, I'd be fine with that."

"Really?!" I could hardly keep the shock from my voice.

"Yes," he said laughing. "Why's that so hard to believe?"

"Well, you've been to Harvard, you're a famous author, you've been on TV. I just assumed you would get bored in Seven Hills. I mean, you did leave immediately after high school."

"High school was a different time. I had an opportunity, and I needed to take it. It was a great experience. I'm glad I did it, and now I'm glad to be home. And I'm not famous, by the way," he said, shaking his head. Ronnie looked down at his desk, slightly embarrassed.

I couldn't help myself, so I pushed a little further.

"Why does it embarrass you when I say that?" I asked. "You are the most famous person from Seven Hills, besides the women accused of Witchcraft in the 1600s. You're very accomplished. You should be proud of yourself. Of those that leave Seven Hills, very few end up somewhere like Harvard."

"That's very kind of you to say," Ronnie said, looking up from his desk. "I guess I don't think of it like that."

We locked eyes for a moment, causing us both to quickly look away. I took a nervous bite of my granola bar.

Ronnie cleared his throat, "Treasure, why didn't you ever leave Seven Hills?" His question caught me off guard. It shouldn't have, especially since I'm the one who asked him first.

"I...um..." just like the morning that I ran into him in the parking lot, I struggled to find the right words. I tried to speak again, but I just shrugged my shoulders. *Again? What is wrong with me? I wanted to say, I feel shackled to my trauma. It grounds me.*

"I'm sorry," Ronnie said, shaking his head, "I didn't mean to make you uncomfortable."

"I'm not uncomfortable...it's just that I never thought I would ever leave Seven Hills. I'm rooted here."

Ronnie seamed to accept that answer, nodding his head in the affirmative.

"I thought that, maybe when Tara left, you and Theodora would have left too." Ronnie stated quietly.

My heart started to beat faster.

"You knew Tara left?" I stammered.

"Of course. My mom and dad still live here. They keep me updated," he explained.

"Oh," I responded, disappointedly thinking about the gossip that must have been going around at the time.

Noticing my reaction, he looked at me quizzically, "Is that wrong?"

"No, it's just, I'm sorry, I don't know," I said, fidgeting in my chair.

I didn't know why that bothered me. There was a question, unspoken, that I wanted to ask. A dark question. Ronnie was so interested in my family. I wanted to ask: *do you think my mother did it? Did she kill my father?* I felt sick again.

"I always asked my parents about you," Ronnie blurted out. "That's why they told me. It's not like they were just filling me in on every little thing that was happening around town."

"Oh!" I blurted, almost laughed.

We both fell quiet, the realization that Ronnie had asked his parents about me at some point while he was away filled every crevice of the room. The mind of a paranoid person is dangerous. Ronnie had been nothing but nice, nothing but amazing. I could feel my body filling with poison. *Why was Ronnie so interested in me, in my family? Was I the person who Ronnie had a crush on in high school? Or was my family his next book?*

At a quarter past nine, Ronnie left his office for the third time to make sure everyone had left the building. Several minutes later, he quietly pushed open his office door and smiled broadly in the doorway. "All clear. Are you ready for this?"

"As ready as I'll ever be," I said nervously.

He held the door open for me as we walked into the hallway. While the building was dark, the security lights in the hallway and those in the parking lot shining through the windows offered plenty of light. When we got to VanHoy's office at the end of the hall, Ronnie removed a set of keys from his pocket and started searching for the master key.

"Okay," he whispered sheepishly, after a couple of long seconds fumbling around. "I guess I should have identified the correct key before leaving my office."

I giggled quietly.

"It's alright," I whispered back. "Next time."

Ronnie chuckled and finally managed to find the correct key. The door creaked open, and we both stepped inside. VanHoy's office didn't have any windows, so it was pitch black. We both turned on our flashlights, and Ronnie partially closed VanHoy's office door. I paused for a moment to still my thumping heart. *It's too late to go back*, I told myself. *You already broke in. Just do what you came here for.* I went to VanHoy's desk and sat in his chair. VanHoy's office was pretty small, and surprisingly neat. There was no clutter, no folders or papers on his desk, and only one photo of him and Mrs. VanHoy. His office computer was missing, with only the monitor and cords left behind, but everything else looked untouched. *Maybe other items have been removed by the police?* On the left wall was a row of metal filing cabinets, and on the opposite wall were a couple of photos of historic buildings in Seven Hills, some old signs, an oversized skeleton key, and an old clock. The display looked rather nice. *I'm sure Mrs. VanHoy had something to do with that*, I thought as I turned my attention back to his desk. I began opening each of the desk drawers and rummaging through their contents as Ronnie started in the filing cabinets.

VanHoy kept several files in the bottom right drawer. I pulled them out individually and carefully began looking through each one, surmising that these were probably the files he accessed most often. I had made it through several files when Ronnie whispered enthusiastically, "Bingo," from the filing cabinets.

"Whatcha got?" I asked.

He brought over some rolled up plans and laid them out over the desk.

"Value Mart plans," he explained, using VanHoy's pen and business card holders to help hold down the paper. "This is how the footprint of the downtown would change after construction."

I followed Ronnie's finger as he explained the differences. Even though I knew Deidra and others were going to lose their businesses, seeing a map of it made me sick to my stomach. Most of the space currently occupied by small businesses would become part of a large parking lot. There was some shading over The Alchemist and other buildings on our side of the street. It was labeled "Phase II."

"What's that?" I asked, pointing to Phase II.

Ronnie removed the top plan, revealing a second, more commercially developed plan underneath. In this version, The Alchemist was gone, and a small strip mall spanned across the space, with even more businesses lost to parking and new construction.

"What?! What?!" I stammered, my eyes darting across the plan. It did not even look like Seven Hills anymore.

"Wow...," Ronnie said, bending over the desk to read the small print. "This wasn't going to stop with the Value Mart. VanHoy had much bigger plans."

"We knew it," I said shaking my head, trying to fight back some tears. "My sisters and I knew there would be more. VanHoy never talked to us about selling. I guess I was hoping we were safe."

"Who knows what will happen now with VanHoy gone," Ronnie said reassuringly. "He seemed to be the only one pushing this project. I know he was also pressuring members of City Council. I'm sure there's an opportunity here to walk this back."

I nodded, wiping a renegade tear. Ronnie carefully rerolled the plans and took them back to the filing cabinets. I finished looking through the files in the desk and let out a loud sigh.

"There's nothing here," I said frustrated. "Do you think the police removed a lot of stuff?"

"I don't think so," Ronnie said turning to face me. "When Nancy told me about the police coming to his office, she said they took his computer. She didn't mention anything else being removed."

"So maybe they encountered the same thing we did? A whole lot of nothing?"

"Maybe," Ronnie replied, shrugging his shoulders.

"This doesn't feel right," I continued. "There's more; it's just not here." I looked again around the office. It was *too* neat and tidy. I'm sure Mrs. VanHoy cleaned the office, and Mr. VanHoy didn't strike me as the type that would allow others to look through his things.

"What are you thinking?" Ronnie asked stepping closer.

"VanHoy was smart. He wouldn't just leave things laying around for his wife, or an employee with a master key to find," I said gesturing to Ronnie. "He'd put it somewhere other people wouldn't have access to it. Am I right? Doesn't this feel wrong to you? Like, it feels staged to me."

Ronnie nodded his head in agreement.

"So, we regroup. Start thinking about other places to which he had access. Maybe his house?"

"I don't know," I said thinking out loud. "I can't imagine he would leave anything where Mrs. VanHoy could possibly find it. She was so against...all of this," I said gesturing to the new city plans. "Their house is probably even cleaner than this office. I don't think he would have taken that risk. Even Sarah said that Mrs. VanHoy would always 'protect her' from VanHoy. Imagine if she had found out all of this information."

"Alright, let's get out of here," Ronnie said, quietly closing the filing cabinets. We both quickly and quietly tidied up the office, checking to make sure everything had been put back in place. After we were satisfied, we tiptoed out, and Ronnie locked the door before we darted back down the hall.

The wind was whipping though the trees, causing the leaves to billow upward like a small tornado. *It's going to rain*, I thought to myself as we exited the front door to the parking lot. I pulled my scarf tighter around my neck and took in a deep breath of the cool night air. I loved a little rain in the evenings in the fall. It was a perfect time to curl up in front of a fireplace with a good book and a glass of wine.

Ronnie escorted me silently to my car. When I got to my door, I turned and smiled. He sheepishly smiled back.

"Thanks," I said. I took a step forward and grabbed him into a hug. His body was tense at first, then he relaxed, and I could feel his warmth all around me.

"Anytime," he said as I pulled away. "We should totally do this again," he added. I laughed.

"Well, if you're game, Dr. Jackman, I'm sure there's going to be plenty of other opportunities. I'm not letting this go. Not until we know what happened to VanHoy. So, I hope any grant funding you have isn't going to be revoked when we are arrested for trespassing." Ronnie laughed out loud, his smile overtaking his whole face.

"I couldn't think of anything more exciting, Treasure."

Chapter 7

"Good morning girls!" Deidra exclaimed happily as she burst through the front door of The Alchemist. She was carrying one of her teal pastry boxes and a drink holder filled with several cups of coffee.

"Mornin'!" I said, bouncing over to help. I put the box down on the front counter and popped open the top. "Oh Deidra!" I squealed happily. Four large cinnamon rolls, dripping with maple frosting and walnuts, stared back at me. They smelled heavenly.

"OMG!" we heard Theo yell from the back; "are those cinnamon rolls?" She burst through the doorway and peered into the box. "I knew it! I thought I could smell it in the air this morning!" Deidra and I both laughed as Theo pulled one out of the box. "Deidra," Theo tried to say, after taking a large bite, "I love you." With her free hand, Theo pulled Deidra into a side hug. Deidra chuckled.

"I know these are a Culpepper favorite. Thought it would get everyone's morning off to a great start!" Deidra said, motioning for me to help myself. She did not have to tell me twice. I pulled a mammoth roll out of the box, then slid it over to Deidra. None of us used forks. These were meant to drip down your hand, just as nature intended, forcing you to lick your fingers at the end. I can only imagine the sounds that were coming from our mouths as we savored every bite of cinnamon roll. An elderly customer walked up to the counter, looking at the three of us.

"You ladies are making an awfully good case for those," she said smiling. The three of us laughed, as Theo took her position behind the counter. She quickly wiped her hands on a towel, hanging off her apron.

"You'll have to excuse us," Theo said laughing. "We take cinnamon rolls very seriously around here."

"I can see that! Do you sell those here?"

"No," I chimed in, "but our friend Deidra here is the baker, and she sells them across the street." Deidra gave a little wave.

"Well, that will be my next stop!" the woman said cheerfully. Theo finished ringing up the woman's purchases. Then, Deidra helped her out the front door, pointing her to Seven Sweets across the street.

"We look like a bunch of animals," Theo said shaking her head.

"Well, we helped make a sale!" I said laughing.

"True," Theo acknowledged.

As Deidra started to come back into the store, she paused, clearly talking with someone coming down the street. She held open the door, and Ronnie walked inside with a hand full of papers.

"Well good morning, Dr. Jackman," I said cheerfully.

"Good morning," he returned, joining Theo, Deidra, and me at the front counter.

"What brings you our way this morning?" I asked.

"Well, I was doing some thinking last night about VanHoy-" he stopped short, noticing the cinnamon rolls on the front counter. "Umm…, is that meant for Tara?"

"Tara isn't here," Theo said, sliding the box over to him. He excitedly pulled the last roll from the box and took a large bite. I laughed at Theo, willing to turn on our sister for the good doctor.

"Oh my," he mumbled with a full mouth, "these are amazing!" We all chuckled.

"VanHoy?" I asked.

"Oh yeah," Ronnie said swallowing. Deidra handed him a cup of coffee. He took a quick sip. "I need to come by more often!" We all smiled. "Okay," Ronnie continued, "so I don't know what Treasure told you about last night-"

"Not nearly enough," Theo said sternly, interrupting him. She looked too much like Mom when she did that.

"All you need to know is that we were trying to figure out if there is a connection between VanHoy and Mills," I responded.

"And we were talking about places where VanHoy may have stored records regarding his 'off-the-books' dealings. His office space is a little sparse, and we don't think he would keep materials where his wife could possibly find them."

"Make sense," Theo said, nodding in agreement.

"He has access to the entire town hall building like all of the staff, but there are a lot of spaces that no one uses anymore, especially in the basement." As he spoke, Ronnie laid his papers on the counter, displaying a floor plan.

We all moved in closer.

"This is what the layout looked like in the 60s, after the last renovation," Ronnie explained. "When the building was first constructed in 1889, it served multiple functions. Pretty much every town service was based out of this building, including the first formalized police department. In fact, in this back corner," he said pointing to the area on the map, "there was a jail cell. Now, this was still being used as a jail cell up until the early 1930s. According to records, one night, while a prisoner was being held there, a fire broke out in the cell. I'm not sure what happened to the prisoner, and the cause of the fire was never determined, but after that, prisoners were no longer kept in that area. The new police station was built several years later, and the area was partially blocked off in the 1960s renovation. But here's the thing; the cell wasn't removed. It had been used for storage, so it was still accessible as a storage area, even after the renovation."

"Okay, so what does this mean?" I asked.

"The footprint has changed slightly since the 1960s; a minor divider wall was removed, but it still looks like this, and, to my knowledge, the jail cell was never removed. That key on the wall in VanHoy's office," Ronnie said looking at me, and I nodded with the memory, "jogged my memory late last night. That's the old jail cell key."

"Oh!" I exclaimed standing straight up. "Do you think that's where VanHoy is keeping records?"

"Wait," Theo interrupted, before Ronnie could respond. "How do you know about some key on VanHoy's office wall?" Theo was totally channeling Mom right now. Ronnie and I looked at each other. "Oh no, Treasure," Theo said, putting her hands on her face. "What did you do?"

"Theo," I said raising my hands, "don't. Just don't. It's better that you don't know."

Ronnie cleared his throat. "Anyway," he continued, "I think it's absolutely possible. He knew about the jail cell. He and I have specifically discussed the fire incident. His grandfather, who was a police officer, was there the night of the fire. I guess his grandfather used to talk about it all the time. He told it as a scary story to frighten the kids."

"Oh, that's lovely," Deidra said sarcastically, rolling her eyes.

"Apple doesn't fall far, as they say," Theo nodded shaking her head in disgust.

"I didn't go down to look this morning because there were a bunch of people in the building. There's a lot of junk down there, but I'm sure if VanHoy was accessing the jail cell, even just once or twice a year, there's probably a path. I think it's worth checking out. At least we wouldn't have to break in," Ronnie chuckled, but then stopped abruptly when Theo's eyes nearly bugged out of her head.

"Break in?!" she barked. Deidra and I both turned quickly to make sure no one else had wandered into the store. "No one else is here!" Theo spit out. "I've been watching. What on earth are you doing? Do I need to call a lawyer?"

"No!" I said shaking my head. "Don't you want to clear our name? Aren't you tired of being under suspicion?"

"Of course," Theo explained, "but while proving our innocence, let's not actually become guilty of another crime. What's the point in that?"

"First of all, no one here is saying that any crime has been or will be committed," Ronnie stated. "Treasure and I can go back tonight and check out the basement. I have a key. I'm allowed to be in the building after hours. I can have guests after hours, as long as they are under my supervision."

"But you need that key from VanHoy's office to get into the jail cell," Theo countered, hands now squarely on her hips. "How are you going to do that?"

"Again," Ronnie said, this time clearly intimidated by Theo, "no one here is saying...."

"Argh!" Theo said, throwing up her hands in disgust. She paused for moment and took a deep breath. "Okay, I won't ask any questions. But promise me you will be careful. This family cannot afford to lose any more of its members. I don't know what the punishment is for burglary, but I cannot accept visiting my sister in prison."

"I don't have a previous criminal history. I'm sure it would just be like, probation," I said jokingly. Theo's left eyebrow popped up. That was a clear indication that she was ticked.

"Ah, too soon, I think," Deidra said shaking her head. "Way too soon, Treasure."

"And you!" Theo said directing her anger towards Ronnie. "What are *you* thinking? You have a lot to lose, *Doctor Jackman.*"

That point caused the air to catch in my throat. I was willing to accept these consequences because it was my family. I couldn't have Ronnie getting in trouble for our problems.

"Ronnie…" I started. "Theo's right. I shouldn't be dragging you into this. This isn't your problem."

Ronnie sighed. "Look, I didn't mean to make anyone upset. Firstly, I am grown man. I can make this decision for myself." He looked at Theo and she nodded. "Secondly," he paused and looked down at the counter for a moment, "I think that the Culpepper sisters deserve some backup. There is a history of disservice here, and the very least I can do is stand by your sides as you try to work this out. I don't just *think* that there are some officers in that department who believe you are somehow connected to crimes in this town; I *know* there are some officers who seriously believe that. I can't know what it's like to be in your position, but I can understand how incredibly frightening that must be."

I felt tears starting to well in my eyes and a cry forming in the back of my throat. I looked at Theo who looked like she too was holding back emotion.

"Like I said," Deidra added, a few tears rolling down her cheeks, "totally Team Culpepper."

"So," I said clearing my throat, "what's the plan?"

Ronnie smiled sweetly. "My office? Say around 8 o'clock?"

At a quarter till eight, I left The Alchemist to meet Ronnie at his office. Tonight, I was a little more prepared for the adventure. I put on some heavier boots and an old flannel shirt and grabbed two pairs of work gloves, newer flashlights, and a battery-operated lantern. Ronnie had said that the basement was filled with a bunch of junk, so I wanted to make sure I was prepared to move things around if necessary. When I arrived, there were still a few cars in the parking lot, so I quickly made my way inside to avoid being seen. Without knocking, I pushed into Ronnie's office door and quickly closed it behind me. Ronnie popped up from his desk with a huge grin on his face.

"What?" I asked.

"Prepared for a night hike in the wilderness?" he chuckled.

"You said there was junk," I said looking over my outfit. "I wanted to be prepared!"

I took one of the pairs of gloves from my rear pants pocket and tossed them to Ronnie. He caught them, then laughed some more as he looked them over.

"Ronnie, are you seriously laughing at me?!"

"Yes," he continued, his chuckle growing into a full-on giggle. "I just...," he started looking down at the gloves, "clearly, I am underdressed for this occasion!"

Ronnie was wearing navy blue dress pants and a brown blazer. And loafers. He looked like a professor.

"Clearly!" I said mockingly. "I expect you to be better prepared for when we go breaking and entering!"

"Um, well..." he said moving towards the closet in his office, "hold up. I think I have some tennis shoes."

As Ronnie puttered around his closet, I dropped into one of the chairs in front of his desk. I could hear a couple of people leaving the building.

"Found 'em!" Ronnie called out, emerging with a very worn set of shoes. He sat behind his desk and started to change out of his loafers. "There now, you see?" he asked, holding up a foot so I could see it in a shoe. "All better!"

"Yes," I said sarcastically. "That makes all the difference in the world!"

Ronnie continued to smile as he shook his head. He pulled out his town hall plans from earlier and spread them over his desk. I moved to the edge of my seat to get a better look.

"Okay," he started, taking a moment to get his bearings. "We're going to enter the basement here," pointing to a shaded area of plans. "It's not super clear on this version, but that is actually a staircase. This is the staircase that's to your immediate right when you enter the building." I nodded with understanding. "So, you already know, there are no doors. It's literally just roped off at this level. When we get to the bottom, there's a small foyer and several doors leading to separate hallways. We need to go through the center one. I peeked down there after I first moved into this building, and I saw a bunch of boxes, old tables, and chairs stacked up, so we'll have to make our way through that mess. The actual jail cell sits in the back left corner of the building." He paused and pointed to the area of the map. "On the outside of the building in the back, you've probably seen what could have been a door, right? It's filled in with bricks?"

I paused for a moment, thinking back about the town hall, when we were kids and used to play in the grass around the building.

"Yes," I remembered. "As kids we always thought it was a secret passageway."

"It kind of was," Ronnie replied. "Back in the day, that was actually a useable door that went straight into the police area of the building. That's the entrance that was also used for any prisoners, so they didn't use the same entrance as the rest of the public."

"Huh," Treasure murmured.

"Yeah, so, when the police department moved into their own building, that entrance was bricked-off, so everyone had to come through the doors on this level. Anyway," Ronnie continued, "that's the approximate location of the jail cell. It's a couple of feet from that entrance, built into the corner of the building. Those two small bricked up windows you can see from the outside were the windows into the cell. At the time, there would have been bars. Officers used to cover them from the outside during the winter and bad weather."

Ronnie started to explain additional features of the outside of the building that didn't actually have anything to do with the task at hand, but I let him continue. He was completely enthralled with the history, and his enthusiasm was catching. I just couldn't help but smile at him, no longer really following his fingers as he referenced certain areas on the plan. Eventually, he felt me staring and stopped abruptly.

"I'm sorry," he blushed. "I get carried away...."

"No, don't be sorry!" I giggled. "You clearly love this place, and it's pretty cool to hear you talk about it. I am absolutely confident that I know the approximate location of this jail cell."

"Okay," Ronnie said with exaggeration, like someone being scolded, his face still slightly pink. "I guess that was a bit much."

"I do want to hear more about the fire, though. Can you tell me more about that?" Just then, there was a knock at Ronnie's office door, startling us both.

"What should I do?" I whispered.

"I, uh–" But before Ronnie answered, his door started to open. I bolted from the chair and stood in the area behind the door. Ronnie's eyes got wide, clearly thinking my amateur hiding place wasn't going to work, but it was too late. The door swung open.

"Hey, Ronnie!" Nancy said, taking a step inside.

"Nan-Nancy!" Ronnie said, awkwardly taking a step back. I tried to make myself as flat as possible and pressed against the wall. I could see Ronnie looking towards me, as he took a seat at the edge of his desk. He quickly looked back at Nancy.

"Is everything okay?" she asked quizzically. "You seem kind of flustered."

"No, I mean, yes, everything is fine. I...I was just caught up in something, and you startled me. That's all."

"Oh, okay...," Nancy replied.

Get it together, Ronnie, I thought to myself.

"Well, I just wanted to let you know that we're all done. I was going to lock the doors on my way out."

"That's, that'll be great, Nancy. Thank you. I think I'm going to stick around awhile longer."

"Okay..." she said hesitantly. "Are you sure you're okay?"

"Yes," Ronnie said, finally mustering some confidence. "Like I said, totally fine."

"A man your age shouldn't spend all his time alone in this old building. You should be going out, having some fun. I heard you were at The Witches Brew the other night with Treasure Culpepper. She's a beautiful young woman, Ronnie...."

Ronnie started sputtering. In any other circumstance, this encounter would have been hilarious, and my sisters and I would have cackled about Ronnie's reaction for days. But now wasn't the time. He looked like he was going to pass out.

"I'm just saying," Nancy continued. "She's a sweet girl. You should ask her out. I think you two would look so cute together. I think all that witch stuff is largely exaggerated anyway."

"Um, thank you, Nancy. I'll take that under advisement," Ronnie said, bouncing up from the edge of his desk to usher Nancy out of his office.

"Oh, okay," Nancy said, walking back through the doorway. "Well, goodnight!"

"Goodnight Nancy." Ronnie waited for Nancy to leave and lock the front door to the building before slowly closing his office door. We stared at each other blankly for a moment, and then I took a large breath, unable to restrict my breathing any longer. Ronnie looked completely dumfounded. I couldn't help myself—I just started giggling.

"Treasure, please," he begged, his face blushing again with embarrassment.

"You're okay, Ronnie," I said, patting him on the shoulder. "Now let's get this thing going!"

This time, Ronnie had VanHoy's office key between his thumb and pointer finger before we ventured into the darkened hallway. We quickly slipped into the office, and I carefully lifted the jail key from its spot on the wall, as Ronnie stood alongside the doorway, allowing some light to filter in. The key was heavy, and I could see where it left a slight mark on the wall where it was hanging. I carefully placed it in my back pocket and headed for the door.

"Task one completed," Ronnie whispered, as he relocked the door. We quickly walked back to the front of the building, to the location of the old staircase. Just as Ronnie had explained, the stairs were blocked by an old, red rope. As Ronnie unhooked the left side, the fastener that held the rope to the banister fell and loudly clinked down several stairs. We both stood in terror for a minute, as the sound seemed to echo throughout the entire building, with Ronnie holding the end of the rope.

"Shit," he whispered.

Hearing Ronnie curse, and with the growing pressure of the evening, I couldn't help myself and started to giggle again.

"Treasure!" he admonished.

"Dr. Jackman, you just said 'shit'," I responded.

"We are never going to find that piece," Ronnie groaned. He carefully laid the rope over the opposite banister and peered down the stairs.

"I'm sure if anyone bumped that rope it would have fallen. It's just old," I reasoned, turning my lantern on low. "Are you ready?"

"Yep, let's do this," Ronnie said, taking the first step down the stairs.

Ronnie and I stood side by side and carefully descended the long, switchback staircase into the basement.

"So, what was the deal with the fire?" I asked again.

"Well, story goes, it was a female prisoner. I haven't been able to confirm the charges through any kind of documentation, but the way VanHoy told it to me, she was brought in for 'immorality.' VanHoy assumed that meant prostitution based upon his grandfather's telling of the story, but for women during that time, it could mean anything from prostitution to walking unescorted through town. It's difficult to know exactly without the records."

"Seriously?!" Treasure replied.

"Yes, unfortunately," Ronnie nodded. "So," he continued, "VanHoy's grandfather is allegedly one of two officers who were on duty that night at the jail. After she's secured in the cell, they left her to play cards in another room. Next thing they know, they see a thick cloud of white smoke rolling in from the hallway. They rush back to the jail cell, fumble around to get it open, and when they finally do get it open, the rack and the desk are on fire. They manage to put it out, and it's only then they realize that the prisoner is gone."

"What?!" I paused on the step and looked at Ronnie.

"Yeah, according to their claims, the woman just disappeared. I mean, I think it makes more sense that, in the confusion, she slipped out the door that was there at the time, but I guess the grandfather swore up and down that the woman did not escape; she vanished. So, then the story gets embellished. This woman is a descendant of local witches and used a powerful spell to break herself out of the jail cell." Ronnie continued, getting into the story.

I zoned out, my heart thumping wildly, as I suddenly remembered an old story my Mom and Aunt Elaina had told us as a child. My mind raced trying to put the pieces together, but I couldn't quite summon up the details. *Had I heard this story before? Was this woman a Culpepper?* Ronnie placed his hand on my shoulder, and I nearly jumped out of my skin.

"Whoa," he said, reaching for my arm to keep me from stumbling down the steps. "I'm sorry, I didn't mean to scare you. Are you okay?"

"Yeah, yeah," I said breathing heavily, "I'm fine, I'm fine."

"Okay," he said removing his hand. "It's just a story. Nothing to be scared about," he teased. "Besides, it happened a long time ago."

We took three final steps and reached the small foyer area. Just as Ronnie had indicated, there were several doors; the one immediately in front of us had a large, glass window that offered an eerie reflection of the two us courtesy of the low light of the lantern. To the left was an older-looking, wooden door, and another wooden door was at the end of a short hallway to the right.

"So, which one will you take, Dr. Jackman?" I stated in a whispered, game-show voice. "Door number one, door number-"

Just then, something banged loudly from behind the second door. Ronnie yelped, and I grabbed his arm, pulling us both into the short hallway on the right side of the foyer. I quickly dimmed the lantern.

"Is someone in there?" I whispered to Ronnie.

"I don't know," Ronnie whispered back, his voice quivering. "I didn't think anyone else was in the building."

We were both panting loudly from fear, each of us trying to take quiet, deep breaths, in an attempt to regain our normal heartbeats. Ronnie moved to the edge of the hallway, and I grabbed his hand.

"What are you doing?" I shrieked. "Don't go over there!"

"I'm not leaving the hallway," he said reassuringly. "I'm just trying to get a better look." Ronnie tried to keep himself as flat as possible against the wall as he peered around the corner.

This was a mistake, I kept thinking over and over again. Then I started fantasizing that VanHoy's killer was actually in the basement, having returned to the jail cell to clean up evidence. As my mind raced, the hallway seemed to get darker and longer. Ronnie inched back closer to me and grabbed my hand.

"What do you want to do?" he asked.

"Do you think someone's in there?"

"I don't know. I can't tell from here. This is a large building. There could be someone in the back and we wouldn't know it," Ronnie answered, his voice clearly strained. He rubbed his face with his free hand. "Or, it could be nothing. Right, it's probably nothing. Right?!" He looked over at me. Even in the dark, I could tell he was looking for some reassurance. I took a moment to calm myself, letting my mind clear so I could truly listen to the space. I heard a couple of clicks, lightly howling wind, and some creaks. *Old building noises,* I told myself. *Yes, nothing but old building noises.*

"Let's keep going," I said, with a surprising amount of confidence. Ronnie nodded.

"Just, just stay behind me," he whispered tightening his grip on my hand. "Seriously, if someone is down here, you run like the wind out of this building and don't look back."

I smiled and squeezed his hand.

"Okay," I whispered.

Keeping our backs to the hallway wall, we slowly inched our way to the foyer entrance. I heard Ronnie take a deep breath before he stepped back into the foyer. I stayed immediately behind him, placing my free hand on his left shoulder. He looked back at me and nodded as he reached the right side of the center door. He peered through the glass, carefully keeping his head off to the side.

"It's too dark," he complained.

I handed him a flashlight.

"Well, I guess if someone sees this, we'll at least have a moment's head start," he reasoned. Ronnie turned on the flashlight and held it up to the glass, slightly illuminating the hallway behind. "Alright, I don't see anything moving," he said after a minute or two. "Are you ready?"

"Yes," I squeaked.

Ronnie slowly opened the door, and we stepped through. The air was stale and musty, smelling like an old library that had been kept in the basement. After a couple of steps, I could feel cobwebs across my face. I tried to wipe them away, but quickly gave up. *Don't freak, don't freak*. After a couple of feet, the hallway opened into a larger common area. I backed off from Ronnie to allow myself a better look at the room. It was filled with junk. There were tables and chairs stacked on one another and file boxes with dates from the last 20 years haphazardly left throughout the space. On one wall, what looked like old elementary school cubbies were filled with additional file boxes, old board games, and vinyl curtains. Despite all the junk, we could move freely around the space. There were clear paths, especially around the newest file boxes.

"It looks like, at the end of every fiscal year, Nancy brings down all of the financial records and just looks for a place to dump them," Ronnie said shaking his head, using the flashlight to read some of the boxes. "This is the worst environment for document storage. Some of these older boxes are probably filled with mold."

"Gross," I said crinkling my nose.

"And some of this stuff we really don't need to keep any more," he continued, popping the lid off a box to look inside. "I guess this spring–" Ronnie shrieked causing me to jump.

"What's wrong?" I said as I rushed towards Ronnie as he was rapidly backing away from the box. We collided and both stumbled, falling into a stack of chairs.

"Mice!" he squealed, using the flashlight to scan the floor.

"Oh, is that all??" I said relieved. I took a step back and grabbed Ronnie's hand to help him regain his balance. "I thought you saw someone."

"That was bad enough," he said, shaking out his clothes and straightening his jacket.

"Did they...like, attack you?" I joked.

"Might as well have," he said sternly. "Don't like mice. Especially don't like mice in file boxes."

"Come on," I said pulling him away. "Let's get focused here."

"Okay, I think we need to enter that door there," Ronnie said, ignoring my teasing and pointing to the left side of the room. That leads to some offices. The cell should be at the end of the hallway."

We slowly made our way to the back left side of the room and entered the identified door. Immediately, we were hit by colder air, causing me to shiver. I tightened my grip on Ronnie's hand. There appeared to be five separate offices in this area, and all of the doors were closed except the fourth one down. I could feel my heart starting to race again as we neared the office with the open door. Just as we passed the third door, the fourth door slammed shut. We both crashed into the opposite wall, and I buried my head into Ronnie's chest.

"Who's there?" Ronnie yelled. "This is a restricted area!" The door slightly popped open, causing us to flee to the end of the hallway.

"Let's get out of here!" I cried, reaching for the doorknob. The fourth door opened even wider.

Ronnie bent down and grabbed an old flagpole that was lying on the floor.

"This is your last chance to come out!" he bellowed, holding the flagpole up in a defensive manner. "Stay here," he whispered to me as he took a few tentative steps forward.

My back felt like it was glued to the wall. As Ronnie neared the fourth door again, I regained my courage and tiptoed behind him. When we reached the door, he forcibly pushed it open and jumped inside. The door slammed against the side wall and bounced back, striking us both. The room was empty, but the culprit was quickly identified. The boards that had been nailed on the outside of the building to cover the old windows had come loose, allowing the cool, fall air to rush into the room with every gust of wind. Ronnie lowered his makeshift weapon and looked over at me. I started laughing. Loudly.

"The wind?! Seriously?!" I howled. "I thought we were going to be murdered."

"Same here," Ronnie stammered. "I'm going to need a drink after all this." Ronnie tossed the flagpole to the ground. "Come on, we're almost there," he said grabbing my hand and pulling me from the room. We quickly came to door number five, and Ronnie pushed open the door. Taking a step inside, I could see additional file boxes, but these were obviously older, some having collapsed under the weight of others. But as I looked to my left, I could see bars between some of the boxes. Ronnie and I started moving boxes out of the way. We moved enough to access the old jail cell. I reached into my back pocket and removed the key. Ronnie stepped out of the way to give me access to the door. As I pushed the key in, my fingers grazed an oily substance around the keyhole. I pulled my hand back and hesitantly put it to my nose.

"What is it?" Ronnie inquired.

"WD-40," I said excitedly.

This was it. This had to be it. Someone had to have entered that cell in the not-so-distant past. Sure enough, the key turned easily, and the cell door swung open smoothly; it too had been well oiled. Ronnie and I smiled at each other and walked inside. There was a desk in the middle of the cell, with additional, newer file boxes lining the right wall. I hurriedly made my way to the seat behind the desk and sat down. Directly in front of me was a deposit slip dated two weeks ago, with VanHoy's name written across the top.

The actual jail cell wasn't as scary as I thought it would be once we were inside. In fact, I found it to be rather cozy. With the glow of the lantern, it felt more like a cabin in the woods than an old jail cell in a damp basement. There wasn't any evidence of the fire long ago. A new rack must have been installed at some point in time, and it had a newer looking, roll-up mattress. I started to wonder if VanHoy came down to the cell to take naps.

With the lantern turned up, Ronnie and I, slowly and methodically, made our way through VanHoy's papers. From a ledger on the desk, it became immediately clear that VanHoy was depositing payments from The Witches Brew made out to Wicking, LLC. Ronnie later found paperwork confirming that VanHoy was Wicking, LLC. This confirmed what we had already suspected: VanHoy was a partial owner. What really surprised us was the amount of money VanHoy had been depositing from the bar: approximately $100,000 a year for the last 13 years. We both agreed that there was no way The Witches Brew generated that amount of business.

"VanHoy and Mills were laundering money," Ronnie explained, after reviewing the ledger and other financial documentation. "They were claiming all this money as profits from the bar and were paying taxes on it, but the money isn't actually coming from the bar. In fact, the actual bar seems to be losing money."

"There are people on the payroll who I don't think ever worked at the bar," I added. Ronnie put the papers he was reviewing on the desk and joined me on the rack. I handed Ronnie a list I'd been compiling. "I'm going through the payroll records and noting every person who's received a check. I heard some of the people on this list tended bar, like David Pewter and Casey Hake. I think they both worked there for a few years. And your former student, Alexis, of course, is in here. But Cliff Bishop? According to these records, he was receiving checks through the end of August."

"Could he be doing maintenance or something?" Ronnie asked.

"If he is, he was making almost $25,000 a year for less than 10 hours of work a week."

"Whoa! That's a pretty nice side gig," Ronnie chuckled.

"But no checks in September or October," I continued. "I'd be pretty upset if I lost that kind of income." Ronnie nodded in agreement. I pointed to another name on the list. "Do you recognize this name?" I asked.

"Sam Lester? Yes, I remember him. He was two classes behind us, right?"

"Yeah, I think so. He's also on the payroll and has been for years. His mom comes into The Alchemist pretty regularly. According to her, Sam works in Boston, but he's also making around $25,000 a year from the bar."

"This is big," Ronnie said stroking his chin. "Like, really big!"

"Yeah," I sighed and closed my eyes for a second. I was starting to go cross-eyed from reading in the low light. I pulled my phone out of my pocket. "Holy crap!" I exclaimed. "It's nearly 1 am!"

"What?" Ronnie said, also reaching for his phone. "Wow. I can't believe we've been down here that long."

"Theo's probably losing her mind. I don't have a signal on my phone." I jumped up and walked closer to the boarded-up windows. It didn't help.

"Okay," Ronnie said surveying the room, "we need to get out of here for now. What are we going to do about this?"

"I think we should take the most important documents with us, just in case someone else knows they're here. I don't want to risk losing them."

"Agreed."

"And um," I started my next sentence cautiously, looking directly at Ronnie to gauge his reaction, "as much as I hate to say it...I think we need to go see Detective Harrison."

Chapter 8

By the time we gathered the papers we wanted and returned the key to VanHoy's office wall, it was 2 am. At that point, we were completely wired and decided to go to an all-night diner several minutes outside of Seven Hills. The location was just off the freeway and offered ample parking to truckers who were looking for a place to park for the night. When we arrived, the diner only had one other patron, a person seated at the counter. Ronnie and I took a seat in the back.

"Good mornin', y'all," the waitress said as she joined us at the table. "What can I getcha?" Her name was Delores, and she had unnaturally red hair, done up in a beehive. Her voice was low and raspy, like she had been smoking for years. Her smile was wide and friendly.

"Can I have a cup of coffee please?" I asked, briefly glancing at the menu.

"Sure thing, sugar. And for you, darlin'?"

"Same here, thank you," Ronnie replied, nervously tapping his foot. Delores walked away, and Ronnie redirected his attention back to me. He hadn't been happy with my suggestion that we go and see Detective Harrison. In fact, after I had called Theo to check in, he spent the entire car ride trying to talk me out of it.

"Do you have a better idea?" I asked, finally breaking the silence in the diner.

"No," Ronnie admitted, shaking his head. "I don't. It just makes me nervous. It won't go well."

"So?"

"So, I guess we figure out how we are going to have this conversation with Harrison," Ronnie stated and shrugged. "We need to get our stories straight. The best thing to do is to keep it simple."

"Agreed," I replied with a half-smile.

At 6:30 am, Ronnie and I left the diner for the police station. At this point, my heart was beating rapidly from a mix of fear and caffeine, and despite the cool air, I was sweating like crazy. After checking in at the front desk, we were taken to a rear office area to wait for Detective Harrison. There were not many people around the police station at that time. It seemed that each person who walked by, gave us a strange look. I met each strange look with a forced smile.

"What a way to start my day." I turned my head to the sound of Detective Harrison's voice. He was wearing his annoyed face and holding a cup of Deidra's coffee. *At least his taste has improved*, I thought to myself.

"Good morning, Detective Harrison," I said a little too cheerfully.

"You must be Dr. Jackman," Harrison said reaching out his hand to Ronnie. "I haven't had the pleasure."

"Very nice to meet you, sir," Ronnie said rising to take Harrison's hand. "Thank you for seeing us so early this morning." Harrison nodded once in reply.

"Alright, Miss Culpepper," Harrison said looking towards me, "we'll meet with you first. This way please," he said motioning down the corridor.

"Wait—what?" I asked startled. "Ronnie and I are here to speak with you together."

"That's not how this works, Miss Culpepper," Harrison replied. "You say you both have new information on the VanHoy investigation? We will interview you separately."

My heart nearly fell to the floor. *Interview?* I looked at Ronnie who nodded his head reassuringly. Harrison took me down the hall to a small room, complete with a metal desk, a two-way mirror, and a video camera. Now, my heart was racing.

"Miss Culpepper, this is Detective Mark Davis, also from the County Sheriff's Office. He'll be joining us this morning." Detective Davis mumbled some greeting, and I reluctantly shook his hand. Harrison sat down across from me and flipped a couple of pages in his notebook. "Are we ready?" he asked. I was about to respond when I heard two knocks on the two-way mirror. A red light appeared on the camera facing the table. I gulped loudly. *What had I done?*

"This is Detective Michael Harrison, badge number 4103, County Sherriff's Office. It is the 30th day of October, two-thousand and twenty-one. The time is 7:14 am. We are at the Seven Hills Police Department, Interview Room 3." Harrison nodded to Detective Davis.

"I am Detective Mark Davis, badge number 4345, County Sherriff's Office."

"This interview is with Treasure Culpepper, who voluntarily approached the police department this morning claiming to have information about a murder investigation. Is that correct, Miss Culpepper?"

"Um...yes," I whispered.

"Miss Culpepper, I am going to need you to speak up for the camera."

"Yes!" I shouted. Detective Davis chuckled and gave Harrison a side-eyed glance. Harrison rolled his eyes up towards the ceiling and sighed slightly.

"Miss Culpepper," Harrison started, pinching the upper bridge of his nose between his thumb and pointer finger, "you can speak in a normal volume. Just don't whisper." I nodded my head in embarrassment.

"Why don't you start by telling us what you found, Miss Culpepper," Harrison resumed.

I took a couple of deep breaths and felt my heart finally starting to slow down. *I can do this*, I thought to myself.

"I've been working on an article with Dr. Ronnie Jackman about Mayor VanHoy for the upcoming festival, so I've been spending some time at the town hall after hours."

Harrison's eyebrows rose slightly. I waited for him to rebuff my statement, but he remained silent.

"We were discussing some of the town's historical sites when he offered to show me the old jail cell in the basement."

"Continue," Harrison said, with a nod.

"Last night, we decided to go into the basement to check it out. When we got down there, we found a bunch of papers that looked like they belonged to VanHoy. The paperwork suggests that VanHoy owned an LLC, Wicking LLC, which we found through a Google search was a partial owner of The Witches Brew. This paperwork suggests that VanHoy and Hansen Mills, who is known to be the owner, were actually in business together."

"Okay, what's your point?" Davis asked impatiently.

"After we found the paperwork, Ronnie mentioned that he sees everyone who comes and goes from the building; his office is right near the front door of the town hall," I continued. "When we first started working on the article, I asked Nancy, VanHoy's assistant, for a copy of his recent schedule. Ronnie noted later that there were a lot of meetings with Hansen Mills that never appeared on VanHoy's calendar." I paused and looked at Harrison. "We were thinking that maybe he got involved in some shady business dealings or something, and that's why he was murdered."

"But I don't get it," Detective Davis said, shaking his head, "why is this business relationship 'shady'?"

Davis leaned forward in his seat and looked over at Harrison. Harrison remained intently focused on me. I found myself starting to sweat again.

"There were payment records in the jail cell," I continued. "Some of them were for people who do not live in this area and for high amounts of money. We took some of the more important records with us. Those are the ones we gave to the clerk this morning. But there are still a lot more down there." Harrison and Davis exchanged glances.

"Well, we don't know anything for sure. It was just an idea," I explained. "Ronnie had remembered seeing the old jail cell key as part of VanHoy's wall decorations, and he and VanHoy had previously talked about the old jail cell, so he definitely had access to it. I know Mrs. VanHoy. She didn't agree with some of the things VanHoy was doing in town. She certainly wouldn't agree with him doing something illegal. Based on what we found, it seems likely that he was using that space to hide things from her and others."

"I see," Harrison responded. He was completely expressionless. I fidgeted nervously in my seat as he made some notes. I started to say more then stopped myself, surmising that it was probably better to say less than try to further explain myself.

"Where is the key now?" he asked.

"I imagine it's still hanging on the wall of VanHoy's office, unless it was removed as part of the police investigation. Or would those things have been returned to Mrs. VanHoy?" I posed, trying to sound as innocent as possible.

Harrison didn't respond to my question.

"So, you didn't go get the key before taking your little adventure to the basement?" Harrison's voice sounded almost like a low growl.

"Why would I? And anyways, we didn't end up needing it," I said shrugging my shoulders.

"How'd you open the jail cell without the key?" Harrison asked, staring intently.

Well, crap, I thought. Ronnie and I hadn't discussed this part of the story. We were more concerned about our reasoning for being in the basement. I could feel panic starting to boil in my stomach.

"I picked the lock with a bobby pin," I stated matter-of-factly.

I winced, instantly regretting my statement. Harrison slammed his notebook on the table, causing me to jump out of my seat. He leaned back into his chair, stretching his arms behind him before folding them across his chest. He took in a deep breath through his nose and slowly exhaled through his mouth. He was furious.

"A bobby pin?! You opened a 19th century iron jail cell door with a *bobby pin*?!"

I held firm. Granted, a bobby pin probably was not the best choice, but I was not going to back down on this, no matter how unbelievable it seemed. I should have said the door had been open, but it was too late now.

"The lock had been lubricated with WD-40," I added.

"Ah, well, that makes all the difference in the world!" he exclaimed sarcastically. I wanted to make a snippy remark back, but again, decided against it.

Harrison dropped his voice down to a more reasonable volume, "How long were you in the jail cell?"

"Almost 5 hours," I responded curtly.

"Seems to me like you should have only needed 5 minutes to determine that those documents belonged to VanHoy and, therefore, needed to be turned over to the police." I didn't respond. "But instead, you and Ronnie decided to take your sweet time and touch every single piece of evidence in that jail cell. Then, you decided to remove some of that evidence and transport it to different locations, isn't that correct?"

My heart sank. It didn't even occur to me that we could be disturbing a crime scene or evidence that was part of the scene.

"Yes," I stammered. "That's correct."

"So, why were you down there so long?" Davis asked in a normal tone.

"We were reading. We– I wanted to make sure we actually had something worthwhile before we came to the police."

"Miss Culpepper, it's not your job to investigate this case!" Davis said raising his voice. "You didn't have to verify anything. That's our job!"

I looked at Harrison, but he just continued to stare and didn't say anything.

"Look, I don't really care if you're angry–"

"This isn't about being angry, Miss Culpepper," Davis explained, leaning across the table. "This is about obstructing a homicide investigation."

I opened my mouth to argue, but Harrison held up his hand to silence both me and Davis.

"What'd you find?" Harrison asked.

"Evidence that VanHoy and Mills were laundering money at The Witches Brew. They-" I stopped abruptly, noticing a sudden change in Harrison's posture and facial expression.

"They, *what*?" Davis asked trying to get me to continue. I looked at Harrison and just had a sense that I should sensor my words.

"Nothing. I mean, that part seemed obvious, but I'm no expert, as you keep pointing out. There were a lot of papers. You'll have to go through them yourself," I said back to Davis.

"You were down there five hours, and you can't tell us more about what you found?" Davis asked clearly annoyed.

"Well, like you said, I'm not a cop." I smiled and sat back in my chair. Davis looked over at Harrison who remained focused on me. I couldn't be certain, but I felt like Harrison was relieved on the inside.

"We're done," Harrison proclaimed, making a closing statement and turning off the recorder. "Miss Culpepper, wait one moment please."

Harrison and Davis both stood and walked to the door. I couldn't quite make out the conversation, but I heard Harrison say that he wanted officers posted at the town hall, but no one was to enter the basement without him. After a couple of minutes, Harrison walked back inside the room.

"Walk with me," he said, reaching for my upper arm. He maintained his grip as he walked me though the station and out a rear door. He released my arm as we reached the sidewalk. We continued walking side-by-side for several minutes before he spoke again.

"I know why you're doing this," Harrison said softly. "In fact, I understand, given your family's history." I stopped walking, and he turned to face me. "Chief Dodd brought me in because he knew he needed an outside person. I know I don't need to tell you that homicides don't happen every day in Seven Hills. This town hasn't seen a homicide in over 15 years. Dodd is the only person in that department who has ever investigated a homicide. It's that lack of experience and general small-town superstition that causes people to come up with crazy explanations when bad things happen. I guess some folks in that department were ready to arrest you and your sisters as soon as VanHoy's body was found."

I clutched my chest at Harrison's reveal. It was one thing to always suspect or fear something was true. But it was something else entirely to hear it confirmed.

Harrison paused, his eyes burning into mine. "Dodd told me about your father," he continued, "that he went missing when you and your sisters were kids. That your mother was a suspect in his disappearance. How nearly everyone thinks that he was murdered. I understand some members of the police department and the town," he said scanning around him, "believe that you girls helped your mother dispose of your father's body. That there was some sort of Witchcraft or Satanic ritual involved." Harrison's voice was even. He sounded sympathetic, much like he did the morning Deidra's bakery was vandalized.

I was never much of a crier, especially in front of other people, but I could feel tears pooling in the corner of my eyes and a lump in my throat threatening to cut off air to my lungs.

"With VanHoy threatening everyone's businesses, threatening Ms. Parker, who is known to be like family to you, there are some officers in that department who are speculating that you and your sisters conjured something up to get rid of him. They already think that you're odd. They think that your family has gotten away with murder in the past, so it's a short walk from that point to thinking that you also had something to do with VanHoy's murder. To be clear, Chief Dodd does not believe any of that. But he knew things could get out of hand if this case wasn't solved quickly and fairly. He was concerned about what the townspeople and the officers in his department could do. He wants a fair investigation. He wants to make sure everyone stays safe."

"But hear me when I say I need you to let me do my job," Harrison said sternly. "There are some parts to this that are only known by me and Chief Dodd. And," Harrison paused briefly and looked around before looking back at me, "one of those things *was* the money laundering at The Witches Brew. Now, that's something the whole department knows. And it will leak out."

"I, I, I'm sorry," I stammered. "I didn't know."

"Of course you didn't know," Harrison chuckled. "You're not supposed to know, okay? That's one of the reasons why you can't get involved. We can't share information, and you don't know how your actions can compromise the investigation. You did the right thing by coming forward. I had been looking for that evidence. But had I known this morning what you found, I wouldn't have brought you into that interview room."

"Well, you could have talked to me first. You know, like a human," I said.

"Yeah, well, I was trying to scare you, so you'd back off," Harrison shrugged.

"But, if you know our history, you know why I can't," I pleaded.

"No," Harrison said putting up both hands, "no more. Treasure, promise me, no more. I know you're scared. But we can't collaborate, and these interferences have major consequences. I don't want to, but I will arrest you if I must. And the more you interfere, the more it makes you look guilty to others in the department. I'm here at the request of Chief Dodd. Things could change, and I could be asked to leave."

I put my hands over my face and sighed. Those tears that had been contained in little pools were starting to roll down my cheeks, but I didn't want to cry in front of Harrison. Sure, he was being decent at this moment, but he also just threatened to arrest me. My head was swarming with mixed emotions. Too much caffeine. Not enough sleep.

"What about Ronnie?" I mumbled.

"We're going to walk back into that department, and you two are going to leave. We're not interviewing him."

"What about the jail cell?" I pressed.

"I got it," Harrison nodded.

"Please, do you have a suspect? When will this be over?"

"I can't tell you. It'll be over soon," Harrison replied with a half-smile.

"I don't think I can stop," I admitted.

"Try harder."

I nodded, and Harrison offered his arm to me. I grabbed on, and we walked back to the police station.

Ronnie and I parted ways, and I ended up back at The Alchemist. I was exhausted, starting to crash from the adrenaline overload, but I wanted to update my sisters before going home. The Alchemist was busy. Both Theo and Tara acknowledged my presence but continued with customers. After about 20 minutes or so, we were finally able to meet at the front counter. I recounted all the details from my night with Ronnie in the town hall basement, to my borderline traumatizing interaction with Detective Harrison that followed. Theo looked worried; Tara was angry.

"Seriously?" Tara angrily whispered since a few customers were still in the store. "There are officers at that station who seriously think we have something to do with VanHoy's murder?"

"Evidently," I responded flatly. "So, our fears weren't unfounded."

"That is weirdly validating and horrifying at the same time," Theo admitted, wringing her hands on her apron.

I nodded.

"I just- I just- Argh!" Tara threw her hands in the air and took off towards the back.

"Tara?" Theo called after her and followed her behind the curtain. "Where are you going?"

Tara grabbed her bag and coat, and without responding, stomped out the back door, slamming it behind her. The force caused some of the items in the back to rattle on the shelves and the customers to briefly look up from their shopping towards the front counter. A moment later, we heard Tara's car and saw her pull out of the parking lot. Theo took a long breath.

"She just needs some space," Theo said mainly to reassure herself. "Treasure, go home and get some rest. You've been up for too long. It's not safe for you to be out and about."

"I'm fine," I said shaking my head, "and I'm not going to leave you at the store alone."

"I can handle this," Theo said firmly. "Go home and text me when you get there. I can't be worried about both of you today. Please?"

Theo's last word was nearly a plea. I agreed, left the store, and headed for home.

As soon as I got to the door of Culpepper Manor, my body began to unwind. My heart rate lowered, and I felt a sense of peace wash over me. I slowly walked up the front staircase to my bedroom, started the shower, and stripped out of my clothes. Once the shower was hot and steamy, I added some lavender and Roman Chamomile into a shower diffuser, then stepped into the water. I closed my eyes as the rhythmic pounding of the hot water grounded me. I slowly ran my hands down my body, releasing my anxiety and sending it down the drain. After my shower, I put on my favorite velvet-pajama pants and oversized sweatshirt, crawled into bed, and instantly fell asleep.

I awoke suddenly, my heart racing from an unknown threat. I grabbed my phone, checked the time, and groaned. I had seriously only been asleep for four hours. I fell back into my bed and tried to go back to sleep, but my mind was racing with a million thoughts. Each time as I was about to fall back asleep, my body would jolt awake, or when I finally managed to fall asleep, a nightmare would wake me up. I tossed and turned for hours. At one point, I heard Theo and Tara return to the house, but I didn't have the energy to get out of bed. My phone chimed, and I grabbed it from the dresser. It was Ronnie.

"Please tell me you're awake and can't sleep either," the text read. I smiled.

"Nice to know it's not just me," I responded. We texted back and forth for several minutes before my stomach started growling.

"How do you feel about midnight pancakes?" I asked, crawling out of bed.

"There's no better kind!" Ronnie replied.

"I agree. Pick you up in 20?"

"See you then."

The only place even remotely close to Seven Hills that was open around midnight was the same diner Ronnie and I had been to the night before. After stopping by Ronnie's house to pick him up, I drove us back to the diner for some blueberry pancakes smothered in maple syrup and topped with several strips of crisp bacon.

"Oh my, this is so good," Ronnie mumbled with a mouth full of pancake. "We should do midnight pancakes more often!"

"We should!" I agreed, wiping some rogue syrup off my chin.

Ronnie and I stayed at the diner for hours, laughing, joking, and telling stories from the past. Ronnie shared a few stories from college, and I filled him in on some Culpepper shenanigans from around the same time period. VanHoy wasn't mentioned. When the rest of the customers cleared out, Delores joined our table and shared stories from her thirty-odd years as a waitress in a roadside diner. My sides hurt from laughing so hard. At around 2 am, Ronnie and I decided we should call it a night. The festival was starting in a just a few short hours, and we both had a long day ahead of us. We thanked Delores and stepped out into the parking lot.

Ronnie and I continued to laugh and joke as we exited the diner and walked to my car. As we got close, Ronnie abruptly stopped talking and grabbed my arm, forcefully pulling me closer and causing me to stop.

"Ronnie, wha-," I started but stopped immediately when I saw Cliff Bishop leaning against the driver's door of my car. Cliff sneered when I finally noticed him, a sly smile slowly appearing on his face. His hands were folded across his large chest, his ankles loosely crossed. Cliff pushed off my car and stood to his full height, causing Ronnie and me to both take a step back.

"What are you doing here Cliff?" Ronnie asked.

"Just thought I'd stop and say, 'hi,'" he said casually. Cliff cracked his knuckles in both hands. In normal circumstances, this would be comically ridiculous; a big, dumb jock, slowly cracking his knuckles to threaten the weird girl and the nerd in the diner parking lot. But tonight, in the nearly empty, poorly lit, parking lot of an out-of-the-way diner, on the outskirts of town, Cliff's actions caused the hair on the back of my neck to stand on end. I could feel Ronnie's hand trembling on my arm. Cliff was still dumb, but the thing that seemed to matter most this evening was his size. Cliff still had a football body, made to look even bigger in the shadows. And he wasn't exactly someone I would consider emotionally stable. The dumb part made him even more dangerous.

"Why are you *really* here, Cliff?" I asked firmly, with a surprising amount of confidence. Cliff chuckled and took a step closer. Ronnie took another step back, but my feet remained planted. *Nope*, I thought. *I'm not backing down to this guy.* Noticing that I wasn't moving, Ronnie took a step forward and now stood slightly in front of me. He dropped his hand from my arm and grabbed my hand, our fingers intertwined.

"You gonna stand up for your woman now, Dr. Jackman? Ooh, I'm scared," Cliff mocked. This time I noticed the slur in Cliff's words. He was drunk.

"Okay Cliff, we're done here," I said stepping forward. I tugged on Ronnie's hand to move towards my car, but Cliff stepped right in front of me. Stale beer breath assaulted my nostrils. "Cliff!" I shouted. "This isn't funny. Ronnie and I are leaving."

"No you're not," Cliff grunted. He reached forward to grab my shoulder, but I pulled back.

"Enough!" Ronnie shouted, this time stepping in between me and Cliff. "Cliff, we're leaving, and if you try to stop us again, we're calling the police."

Cliff chuckled.

"Ronnie, if you knew what's good for you, you'd mind your own fuckin' business."

"What are you talking about?" Ronnie asked.

"You know what I'm talking about," Cliff snarled, putting a finger in Ronnie's chest. "One word and we'll get your Satan-worshiping girlfriend put behind bars."

Cliff never touched me, but his words felt like a punch to the gut. I remembered my conversation with

Harrison. I tightened my grip on Ronnie's hand. Cliff took a step back and gave a creepy smile.

"Now, you two have a pleasant evening." He turned and walked towards his truck. It was parked between two tractor trailers in the extended lot.

"Get in the car," Ronnie said pushing me forward. I scrambled to get my keys from my purse and hurriedly opened the door. When I was in, Ronnie manually locked my door, pushing it closed, and ran to the other side. I started my car, just as Cliff was pealing out of the parking lot.

"What the hell?!" I shrieked.

Because there is nowhere else to go at 2 am in Seven Hills, and neither one of us felt safe staying at the diner, Ronnie and I ended up back at The Alchemist. I triple-checked the door and window locks when we got into the building. Ronnie collapsed into our favorite wingback chair, and I started pacing the floor.

"What the hell?!" I shrieked again. "What was Cliff talking about? Was he following us?"

"Looks like it," Ronnie admitted. "How else could he have possibly known we were at the diner?"

"This all comes back to VanHoy, right? Am I nuts?"

"You're not nuts," Ronnie said shaking his head.

"What if we had this all wrong," I asked biting my bottom lip. "What if VanHoy's murder has absolutely *nothing* to do with the money laundering at The Witches Brew?"

"What do you mean?"

"Just because he was involved in criminal activities, doesn't mean that was why he was killed. Cliff said, '*we*.' '*We'll* get your girlfriend behind bars.' Who is '*we*'?"

"I don't know," Ronnie said, popping out of the chair. He grabbed at his chin as he started to pace next to me. "I mean, Cliff knows everyone. It could be anyone!"

Suddenly it came to me, a shiver running down my spine. Why had I not thought about this before? It makes perfect sense!

"Who would Cliff do anything for? Who would he threaten someone for? Potentially *kill* someone for?" I asked. Ronnie shook his head, not following.

"*Sarah Tarleton*," I continued. "Cliff would do something like that for *Sarah Tarleton*." Ronnie stopped pacing, the color draining from his face.

"Do you think Sarah…."

"Murdered VanHoy," I finished. "Or got Cliff to do it! Think about it," I continued. "VanHoy was killed right in the middle of the downtown festival set-up. I know there are a lot of volunteers, but none of them are ever there that late at night. The only people likely to be down there that late are the festival organizers. The ones working late to get everything ready. Sarah could have been down there. She and VanHoy didn't get along. He was a threat to the festival. The festival that is *everything* to Sarah. What if VanHoy went down there to confront her? Or was just down there antagonizing people? Since it was late, I betcha Cliff was there too, probably lurking in the shadows."

"Okay, okay," Ronnie nodded resuming his pacing. "So, Sarah and VanHoy argue? Cliff steps in and hits VanHoy on the back of the head?"

"Right! Why not?" I asked, throwing my arms in the air. "Think about his behavior tonight! And Sarah has a temper! I've seen her hit people before!"

"I think we all have," Ronnie nodded in agreement.

For everything Sarah Tarleton had, she was a bully. An aggressive, physical bully, who manipulated her friends and got her big, football-playing boyfriend to do her bidding. I thought back to all of Sarah's nasty behaviors in high school and to how she treated Kristy Pickles.

"Even if Sarah didn't do it herself, she had Cliff to do it for her. All she would have to do was ask."

"They know we've been asking questions," Ronnie said, dropping back into the chair. "They must think we are on to them."

"Right," I agreed. "So, what do we–" my question was interrupted by loud banging on the front door. Ronnie and I both jumped, Ronnie leaped back up from the chair to stand next to me. The person outside banged again. I grabbed a wooden cane from a display and held it out like a sword. The blinds were closed over the windows, so I couldn't see outside.

"Do you have your phone?" I whispered to Ronnie.

"I left it in the back," he responded.

The banging happened again, but this time accompanied by a voice: "This is Detective Harrison! Is someone in there?!"

I lowered the cane and looked at Ronnie quizzically.

"Yeah, yes!" I shouted. "This is Treasure. I'm in the store."

"Well, are you going to let me in, or are we going to continue shouting through the door?"

I placed the cane back into the display then went towards the front door. I carefully slid the curtain to the side to confirm it was Detective Harrison. When he saw me, he gave me a stunted wave. He was already wearing his annoyed face. I unlocked the door and slowly pulled it open.

"Why are you here at 3 o'clock in the morning?" he asked, practically pushing himself inside. "I hope you're..." he stopped when he saw Ronnie. "Oh, Dr. Jackman...didn't see you there."

"Detective," Ronnie said nodding in acknowledgment.

Harrison looked slowly around the store. Every time that I'd seen Harrison, he had been in a suit or otherwise dressed up. Tonight, he was wearing an old pair of jeans, a faded blue button-down shirt, and a zip-up vest. His shirt was slightly tucked in on the right side, revealing his gun in a pant holster and his portal radio in his back pocket. Carhartt boots, tousled hair, overnight scruff—he looked...*different. Just different.* Almost normal.

"Why are you in the store this late?" Harrison asked me.

"I didn't know I had a curfew," I snapped back.

"Stop, Treasure, stop!" he commanded. "This isn't funny, what are you two doing?"

"I'm not being funny," I responded. "Ronnie and I were out getting pancakes, and we…" I paused, looking at Ronnie for guidance.

"'We' what?" Harrison asked.

"We ran into Cliff Bishop outside of the diner, you know the one passed the old salvage yard? Well, not ran into so much as Cliff was following us. He threatened us."

"What do you mean Cliff threatened you?" Harrison asked, walking further into the store. Ronnie came up beside me, and we proceeded to tell Harrison the story of our encounter with Cliff.

"I promise," I concluded, "we were not up to anything other than pancakes. This was seriously about a midnight snack."

"Well, your midnight snacks seem to be more eventful than mine," Harrison snorted. "Okay, so why are you at The Alchemist?"

"We're at The Alchemist because we were freaked!" I explained. "And I own this place! What are you doing here?" I demanded, pointing my finger at Harrison. "Are you following us too?!"

"You do remember that we had a murder in the town square just a couple of nights ago? There are extra patrols all over this area," Harrison said calmly. I momentarily felt a little silly. Of course, there would be extra police in the area.

"One of the units reported seeing activity at The Alchemist," Harrison continued, placing his hands on his hips. "So no, I wasn't following you. But you've pulled some really interesting stunts since the murder. I'm trying to investigate a homicide and keep tabs on whatever you and your partner are up to, so when I heard the report over the radio, I decided to check it out myself. I told you to stop investigating this case!"

"We weren't investigating anything!" I yelled. "Tonight had nothing to do with VanHoy until Cliff showed up in that parking lot. But now-"

"Now what?" Harrison interrupted. "What are you going to do now?"

"Look," I continued, "I know you don't want to hear this, but I think Cliff and Sarah Tarleton had something do with VanHoy's murder."

Harrison closed his eyes and dropped his head to the floor, pinching the bridge of his nose with his thumb and pointer finger. I was beginning to recognize that as his go-to move when he was frustrated, his own personal time-out. Before he could interrupt me or ask additional questions, I blurted out my reasons for thinking Sarah and Cliff had something to do with VanHoy's murder. Harrison listened, hardly moving.

"Are you done?" he asked when I stopped talking.

"Yes," I responded.

"Just so we're clear, less than 24 hours ago, you were in the police station, suggesting to me that Hansen Mills had something to do with VanHoy's death. Now, you're suggesting that Cliff and Sarah had something to do with it?"

I didn't know what to say. It sounded like I was all over the place because I was all over the place.

"So, now someone else murdered VanHoy? What do you expect me to do with this? Just start arresting everyone you suspect? You point your finger, and that's the direction I look? Is that what you want?"

"Well, no, of course not," I snapped back.

"Explain this to me," Harrison said taking another step forward. "Why is it that VanHoy, who can threaten anyone in town, was threatened by *you* and *your sisters*? I heard that he'd been in and out of every single one of these shops multiple times, but he stayed out of this place. Why is that?"

My anger blossomed into fury. I took another step towards Harrison; our faces were just several inches apart.

"VanHoy was afraid because he knows what we're capable of," I said between clenched teeth. Harrison's eyes widened slightly for a moment. I had startled him.

"Treasure, do you know something about the disappearance of Jasper Alden or the murder of Silas VanHoy? If you do, you need to tell me now."

There was just something about hearing my father's name from the lips of others that was heartbreaking. The fury that had suddenly consumed me had just as quickly left. I immediately felt empty and alone. I felt like a sad, scared little girl who didn't understand what had happened to her father or why everyone was so angry at her mother.

"No," I breathed, starring straight into Harrison's questioning eyes. "I don't have any direct knowledge of either of those cases. I am telling the truth about what happened tonight. We went to the diner for late night pancakes and a break from all the drama. Something is going on with Cliff, and I think Sarah is somehow involved."

Harrison took a few steps back and rubbed his eyes with his palms.

"I seriously don't understand this town," he moaned. "A homicide in the middle of the town square with no witnesses, money laundering in a shitty bar, a missing person cold case that keeps being brought up, and a set of witches with their academic sidekick! I mean, Jesus Christ! You had it right when you said drama, Treasure."

"Detective Harrison," Ronnie started, but Harrison quickly threw up his hand to cut him off.

"I seriously don't fucking care. I don't even want to hear it."

Just then, Harrison's radio cracked with an officer calling in a stop of a drunk driver. Harrison grabbed the radio to turn it down, but then we all heard Cliff Bishop's name. Harrison turned the radio up to listen. Cliff had been stopped, not far from the diner by a sheriff's deputy. Although I didn't understand all of the codes, it was pretty clear that Cliff had gotten into a fight with the deputy and tried to flee the scene on foot. I looked up at Harrison and caught his eye. *Told you he was drunk*, I thought to myself. Harrison strode over to the door and pulled it open.

"First, I'm going out to this stop. Then I'm going to solve this case," he said facing the street. He paused, then turned to face me and Ronnie. "I don't want to see either of you ever again."

Chapter 9

Today is October 31st. Halloween. Samhain. Today, the veil between this world and the next thins. The day of the All Hallows' Eve Parade and Pageant. I should have been excited, but I could barely get out of bed. I had slept fitfully, plagued with nightmares. Harrison appeared again and again in my mind's eye. He was angry. He accused me of murdering VanHoy. He accused me of murdering my father. He even accused me of murdering my mother. In the dream, I had helped my mother bury my father, just as the rumors reported. Theo, Tara, and I buried him in the backyard of Culpepper Manor in our lush garden, even thicker and greener in my unconscious state. We were all adults in the dream. Standing under a bright full moon, we chatted politely as we piled dirt on his dead body. Unnoticed, Sarah Tarleton had arrived at some point during the process. She put the last pile of dirt on the mound. When I looked at her, she winked, her eyes shining like two bright blue flames in the moonlight.

"His wife did it," she said, resting her arm on the shovel. "His wife did it."

With that, I had awoken with a gasp. I thought about writing the dream down in my journal, my Book of Shadows. However, I wondered if the police found it, would they take it as admission of guilt, should they ever decide to come after us? No other evidence; just the book's confession. If my book was found, I, along with my sisters, might be 'burned at the stake.' No time to collect the cow's tongue or a black velvet purse.

I finally checked my phone as I tried to collect my wits. 9 am. I only had four hours of sleep, none of which were uninterrupted. I hated mornings like this. I woke up feeling *dread*. There was a tightness circling my chest. One false move and my chest could burst open, my heart falling into my lap. Getting dressed, putting on my shoes, and heading out the door took every effort that I had.

The morning was unseasonably cold, and a thick layer of fog covered the road. As I drove towards town, I watched Culpepper Manor and the lush trees surrounding it fade in the rearview mirror. My stomach lurched at the sight of the thick greenery. I had an urge to turn around, race to the back yard, and check to make sure there was not a fresh mound of dirt.

By the time I arrived in town, I had to drive around the area a few times to find a parking spot. I finally found one about a block from The Alchemist. As I headed to the shop, I felt as if I was sleepwalking. Every step took considerable effort. When I arrived at The Alchemist, it was already busy. Theo was posted behind the counter, and it looked as if Tara and Deidra were helping customers. Deidra had recently hired more employees at Seven Sweets and must have felt comfortable spending a little time over here today to help us out.

As I made my way through the crowd, I waved at Deidra. She smiled slightly at the gesture, but a look of concern was etched on her face. With my shoulder, I pushed open the door to the back room and was startled by the presence of Ronnie. He was sitting on a stool at the large commercial countertop in the middle of our back room. The old countertop was covered with every herb, concoction, and decoration under the sun. It looked as if Ronnie— more likely Theo—had made a little space at the counter for Ronnie. He seemed to have taken full advantage, as his elbows were resting on the counter, with his head in his hands. Next to him sat a tall coffee and an untouched cinnamon roll. For a second, I thought he might be asleep.

"Ronnie?" I asked quietly.

He turned on the stool and looked up. "Treasure," he said happily, but wearily. "Hey. Hope you don't mind. Your sisters said I could 'hide' back here until I have to be ready for the parade."

"Of course, I don't mind," I said, sitting on the stool next to him.

We both slouched forward then, resting our heads in our hands. He turned to look at me. He looked tired, but still, he grinned widely. Ronnie had an almost boyish quality about him. He was handsome, tall, academic, almost elegant. Yet, he seemed to have such a love for mischief. I thought about the glee in which he tried to and wanted to 'solve the mystery' with us. His love for 'mischief' must be why he was so interested in the occult, in us, in our family. I wondered why I had never really noticed Ronnie and all his complexities before. Without thinking, I put my hand on his back, smoothing the wrinkles out of his white shirt. He looked disheveled, like he had slept in the garment.

"You need an iron," I commented, as he turned to look at me again, a bright smile appeared on his otherwise tired face. I smiled back at him. I wondered if this was what he looked like in bed in the morning. I shook the thought away; and as I did, he unexpectedly grabbed my arm and pulled me into a hug. The hug was surprisingly intimate. Still seated, he folded his arms around me, his chin resting on the top of my head. It was probably the fatigue, but this felt natural, normal, like he had held me like this a thousand times before. I slipped my arms from my side to around his waist.

"I don't want to go to the parade," he confessed. He cleared his throat, "I want to stay here...stay with you."

I sat back up on the stool, sliding my arms slowly away from around his waist. I needed to pull myself together. Everything felt dulled. I did not know how to process this act of intimacy or anything else that had happened lately.

"I know," I replied, with another smile. Then redirecting the conversation, I continued, "what time do you have to be there?"

He looked at his phone and replied, "Probably now. I know that this year they wanted to work on the sound. So, we don't have another…you know…repeat of previous years."

I nodded and then Ronnie continued, "I wanted to talk to you about something. I was thinking about last night, all night and all morning. Don't you think it's weird that Cliff knew that we were…you know…looking into VanHoy's murder?"

"I hadn't really thought about it," I answered honestly. "I feel like my brain is fried."

He laughed softly, "Yea, me too. But, after we left last night, I kept thinking about Cliff. There is no way he could have known that."

"Unless someone told him," I stated, flatly, picking at a bright-orange, jack-o-lantern cutout on the counter.

"Exactly," Ronnie answered.

"Who could have told him?" Now, my brain fired into action. "You don't think Harrison…"

Ronnie shook his head and interrupted, "I considered that, but he's from out of town. I can't imagine he's involved with this. But what if…someone *else* in the police station is *involved* in this. That person could have told Cliff. You know, tipped him off. Or maybe, one of the police officers working on the case just gossiped to Cliff about the situation. I'm not really sure about the professionalism amongst a lot of the…well…'professionals' around here."

I let out a long breath and put my head back into my hands, abandoning the jack-o-lantern craft.

"I feel like I can't even think about this today," I said, wearily. "Plus, we have so much work to do today. I can't let Theo and Tara do everything all by themselves. Deidra will have to get back to Seven Sweets soon…"

"I know. I should probably go." Ronnie stood up and stretched slightly. He paused for a second, looking down at me and then around our workspace. "It's nice…what you have here."

"I know, it really is," I answered. Recent events had clarified this more than ever to me. I wanted to keep this life. "You better go. If you don't, Mrs. VanHoy might kill you."

"She might," he chuckled. And with that, he got up and exited.

The Alchemist was packed with people. I was not sure if it was busier than usual or if I usually had more sleep prior to working the Halloween rush. I was caught a few times resting in our favorite plaid wingback chair before Tara reminded me that I had slept later than she, and she *could not* remember a single time that we ever allowed her to get extra sleep before a busy holiday workday.

Around noon, the parade began. Theo ushered the customers out to watch, with Tara and I in tow. We stood outside The Alchemist as we had seemingly a thousand Halloweens before. It was a perfect Halloween day. It was still chilly, but the sun shone brightly. The leaves on the trees had turned to beautiful oranges, yellows, and reds, stark against the bright blue sky. The smells from Seven Sweets hung in the air. All around us, onlookers held cups of

Deidra's pumpkin spice blend or some variety of pumpkin pastries, as they watched the festivities begin. I breathed in the sights and smells, trying to soak it all in, to preserve it forever. Seven Hills was nostalgia in a downtown square.

By the looks of the first couple of floats, Mrs. VanHoy had gone above and beyond. The first float held a giant orange and black balloon archway, with a banner that read "Seven Hills' All Hallows' Eve." On the float, there were hay bales topped with jack-o-lanterns of every shape and size, each one carved to perfection. The next float was constructed by Seven Hills High School. It had a 'haunted high school' theme. On the float were high schoolers dressed up as vampires, witches, and ghosts. Sporadically, the kids would spring out from hollowed-out lockers, yelling and throwing candy to the crowd. It was not long after this float that Ronnie came down the street. His float was decidedly less decorated, more serious, more academic, with a just a few bales of hay and a couple of pumpkins. As he sailed by, he relayed the story of the witches of Seven Hills to an enthralled crowd. Luckily, his microphone was working perfectly this year. He was animated and in his element. He looked at me and waved, never missing a beat in his narration.

As I waved to Ronnie, I noticed Harrison standing across the street. Watching. A tightness formed in my stomach. I suddenly felt very aware of myself. I was sure that I must have looked disheveled. I tried hurriedly to smooth my hair down. I felt a sudden urge to alert Theo and Tara and to run back into The Alchemist, shutting the door on the world behind us.

Yet, I would not. This was our town. I stared back at Harrison, abandoning my hair and looking at him straight in the eyes. As I did this, his face softened to an expression that I could not quite read. Eventually, I lost sight of him. As the parade continued, he melted back into the faceless crowd.

The parade was a success. Theo, Tara, and I chatted about the different floats when we got back inside The Alchemist. We took care of all the odds and ends for the All Hallows' Eve Pageant. Luckily, we had finished all the orders even with all the craziness of recent days. Now, it was just a matter of ensuring that all materials for the pageant had been delivered.

"We still have the box that Mrs. Van Hoy left here," Theo said, putting the big box on the high counter with some effort. "She'll need it for the pageant."

"Treasure can take it," Tara interjected from a cross-legged position on the floor. She had one of our many tarot decks spread out on the antique rug. As she spoke, she did not look up, but flipped cards casually. "I need a break, and she got a thousand this morning. Plus, she came in late."

I looked at her and glared, "Is this what we are doing today?"

"Yea," she responded with a smirk.

"Take the box, Treasure," Theo said, shaking her head at Tara. "Tara and I will take a break for lunch and meet you at the pageant. Then, I plan to lock this place up for the rest of the day so that we can celebrate."

I snorted, "Yea, celebrate."

"Just try. Both of you," Theo said, exasperated. She looked tired and worn. We were all tired and worn. After this week, I needed to lay in bed for a month. Tara turned up another tarot card and looked up at us.

"Look," she said, a stoic expression on her face. She raised the card up so that we could see. "It's the Tower."

Theo, Tara, and I exchanged glances. The Tower tarot card often symbolized disaster. A chill ran down my spine.

"I've got to go," I stated.

I grabbed the box from the counter and walked the block to my car. By the time I reached my vehicle, I was exhausted. I drove towards town square. People, cars, vendors, and Halloween decorations now littered the surrounding streets. I imagined the square as a snow globe that someone had shaken and set aside, everything in the tiny world falling into chaos.

I parked and exited my car, in awe of the spectacle. I grabbed the box, which took considerable effort, and began walking towards the town square gazebo. It looked incredible. The gigantic purple and black balloon spider, that Mrs. VanHoy and Sarah had worked on so hard, was perfect. On the gazebo, there were massive spider legs and even spider 'eyes' made from black and white balloons. Just beneath the eyes, two large gleaming white fangs hung at the entrance. Even at a distance, I could see many people inside the structure. No doubt, townspeople and tourists alike, sat at the worn picnic tables, munching on homemade fall goodies of all varieties.

Around the gazebo sat every kind of vendor booth you could imagine. One vendor sold handcrafted masks and costumes. Another passed out brochures for the local bed and breakfast, Seven Hills Inn. Another booth nearby sold elephant ears and Dutch-apple waffles. My mouth began to water, and I suddenly realized just how hungry and thirsty I was.

"Treasure!" I heard a voice call. I turned to see Paul Richards sitting at a booth of his own.

"Paul," I responded, walking over to his booth. "This looks amazing!" And it did. Paul had Halloween crafts of all shapes and sizes. My favorite was the paper decorations adorned with traditional green-face witches, warts and all. As a child, I could remember these appearing in my classrooms, signifying the beginning of the season. I had loved them; but now I wondered about this depiction of witches.

"Did you make all of these?" I asked.

"Most," he responded with a jolly chuckle. "How are things over at The Alchemist today?"

"Pretty good. I mean busy...you know how it is. Hey...have you seen Mrs. VanHoy? I have a box for her."

He shrugged his shoulders. "I haven't seen her once today. And I got here early. Pauly is 'manning' the shop for me. He's pretty excited about it," he paused and smiled. "Maybe ask Mike, or Pat, or one of the others?"

"I will," I answered. "That is really cute about Pauly. I hope it goes well today."

"Thanks. You too."

Waving goodbye to Paul, I turned on my heels and continued to weave through the crowd, a task made more difficult by the large and cumbersome box. My arms began to ache. Since I had arrived, the square seemed to only get more crowded. For a minute, I felt like I could not breathe. I put the box down and squatted, trying to catch my breath.

"Treasure," a voice said, and I lifted my head to see the face of Detective Harrison. "You alright? Do you need help?"

"No," I exclaimed, almost shouting. I jumped to my feet. "Have you taken to following me now? Is that what is going on?"

"No," he said softly.

He motioned for me to lower my voice and looked at me cautiously.

"Please, I just happened to see you here, and I honestly just wanted to talk to you. I didn't follow you. I am here for...uhm...other reasons. Can we talk?"

I said nothing and did not move. I just stared at him, the crowd whirling around us, blurring in the background.

"I'm sorry about last night," he said softly, kindly. It was a tone that I was not used to hearing from him. It made me think of that night at The Witches Brew. The night I wanted so desperately to lean on him.

"You know, what I said. I shouldn't have said it. *I didn't mean it*. I almost came over to your house this morning to apologize, but I thought maybe that wouldn't be appropriate." He looked down at the ground, grinding his foot into the earth. "I'm just...frustrated with this place, with the situation, with *you*, with your family..."

He looked exasperated. He also looked like he had not slept. Even despite his fashionable dress, he did not seem quite as polished as he usually did. It looked like he hadn't shaved in days.

"I'm sorry if *we*, if *this* place, all of it," I responded coldly, a fire rising in my chest, 'frustrates you.' I gestured to the crowd as if to highlight the ridiculousness of it all. *This place, this warm and cozy place, frustrates him? What is wrong with him?*

"No, Treasure, please. You misunderstand me."

"Then, what? Then, *what*?!" I demanded, looking him straight in his bright blue eyes. "*Then, what*?!"

"I just...I honestly just wanted to help you. And apologize...for my behavior. You know that I care about you...as a citizen...," his voice trailed off.

"I'm sorry?!" I asked, bewildered. I choked out a dry laugh. "You care about *me...as a citizen*?"

"I'm sorry," he said, a flash of embarrassment crossing over his face. Since I met him, this was the first time that his expression was transparent. He ran his large, square hand through his dark hair. "Dammit. I'm sorry."

I said nothing; I just stood and stared. I felt my stomach lurch from hunger, thirst, and something unidentified.

"I have to go," I said, looking down at the box as I picked it up. "Mrs. VanHoy needs this box."

"Treasure, let me..."

"I have to go. Don't follow me," I demanded fiercely.

"I wasn't going to follow you," he responded defensively. "Treasure…"

I did not wait to hear what he said. I took off faster than before, weaving in and out of the crowd. I occasionally knocked into someone, barely stopping to apologize. When I finally reached the sidewalk, I felt spent. I wanted to stop, sit on the box, and cry from fatigue. Instead, I pushed my body forward until I got to my car. My mouth was so dry that it felt as if it was lined with cotton. I looked around my car for a liquid of any kind. I even wedged my hands and arms under the seats in the odd chance a rogue water bottle had fallen and had been forgotten. Giving up, I took off towards Mrs. VanHoy's home. *I'll stop somewhere—anywhere—on my way home to get a drink*, I told myself.

Just five minutes had passed before I arrived at VanHoy's estate.

Once, as a child, I attended a Christmas party there. The VanHoy's frequently threw parties, but my sisters and I were always too young to attend. This was not to say that my mother or aunt attended those parties, but that we understood that the frequent parties at the VanHoy's were adult parties. This particular Christmas party was the rare *family* party.

In all reality, the party was probably a fundraiser for one of VanHoy's many campaigns. But in my child brain, the party felt like the most exciting event in my life. For what seemed like forever, I waited in anticipation of the day. My mother and aunt bought Theo and I matching red velvet dresses and new shoes from a now-bankrupt super center a town or two away. The shoes I could remember even more clearly than the dress. They were so shiny; I could see my blurred reflection when peering into them. Tara had not yet been born.

The Christmas party was much grander than I could have ever imagined. Christmas carolers, wearing full 19th century caroler regalia, greeted us at the door. Each one held a giant copper bell that would chime each time the wind blew. I was mesmerized. The memory of the rest of the party was less clear, but I do remember dozens of Christmas trees, eating more frosted cutout cookies than one ever should, and even presents handed to us by a 'Santa Claus' in a plush velvet suit.

Since the Christmas party, I had been to the VanHoy's on just a few occasions to make deliveries. However, every time I came upon it, I was struck by the absolute beauty of the estate. Now, as I pulled onto the long driveway, I marveled at the enormity of the property. Hickory trees with leaves of all colors stood proudly next to the house. Some had probably been there for over a hundred years and had watched the land change throughout time.

The house itself was just as spectacular as the land, a large brick home composed of several spacious stories. It was almost museum-like. On the left side of the home was a large sunroom. On the right side of the house was a gazebo-style porch. Stone lined every corner of the structure, and in the middle of the home was a large stone porch, held in by a stone fence of thick, vase-like cylinders.

When I neared the house, I parked on the right-hand side as to not obstruct the other cars parked along the circular driveway. I quickly hopped out of my car and dug out the box from the backseat. My back 'groaned' as I shifted the box to the edge of the car. I suddenly felt extremely hot and sweaty, despite the cooler weather. Once inside, I would ask Mrs. VanHoy for a glass of water. Grabbing the box, I approached the door, which I was surprised to find wide open. Leaves had blown in from the porch, and tiny fragments could be seen scattered inside on the otherwise spotless and gleaming wood floors. Momentarily forgetting my fatigue, my heart began beating in my chest. Something did not seem right.

"Hello!" I called still standing on the stone porch. "Hello?"

I heard shuffling inside and muffled voices.

"Hello!" I called again, tentatively putting one foot inside the structure. I quickly examined the driveway. A few cars were parked haphazardly. These cars did not seem like they belonged at the VanHoy's. They were *cheap* cars. *Old* cars. Not classically old or vintage cars, but junky, dingy cars.

I could feel my heart pick up the pace again. I took another step into the estate. In the large foyer, aside from the scattered and tattered leaves, nothing looked amiss. A large, chestnut table stood adorned with, what I could only assume was, the Chinese Cloisonne Hu-Form vase. I only remembered the name because Mrs. VanHoy had come into The Alchemist asking for a natural cleaning agent that would maintain the vase's integrity. Eavesdropping, Kristy Pickles had approached us after Mrs. VanHoy left. According to her, the vase was an import, worth tens of thousands of dollars. "A total wealth-flex," she had said, a smug look on her face.

"Hello!" I called again, this time my voice sounded less confident than the times before. "Mrs. VanHoy? Are you alright?"

I set the box near the table and started working my way down the hallway towards the muffled voices. I stopped outside of the door, listening to Mrs. VanHoy's voice arguing with two other voices. Male voices. I opened one of the French doors which led into what seemed to be a parlor. Mrs. VanHoy and the two men all turned abruptly to look me, their mouths agape.

"What in the wor—" said one of the men, his thick sunburnt arms in a cut-off t-shirt.

"Treasure!" exclaimed Mrs. VanHoy, blinking hard several times. It was as if they all saw a ghost.

"Treasure?" asked the smaller man.

I immediately recognized him; It was Jimmy Dickson. He looked casual in a pair of jeans and a white T-shirt, a stark contrast from his usual uniform.

"Jimmy?" I looked at him, incredulous. It was as if we were all conducting some sort of shock roll call.

"Who the hell is this?" said the other man, folding his large, red arms over his chest.

"Mrs. VanHoy, I brought your box," I said quietly, ignoring him. My brain fired rapidly, trying to understand the scene before me. Jimmy and the other man could not look more out of place standing with Mrs. VanHoy in the ornate parlor. Both looked rough, *unkempt*. As he swayed side to side, I suspected the larger man might even be a little intoxicated.

"Are you okay?" I asked Mrs. VanHoy.

"She's fine," said the thicker man, his voice menacing. His sunburn was so bright, it made my own skin feel on fire.

I could see small circles of peeling skin on both of his upper arms. In the light of the parlor, it looked as if he was molting. I shuddered. And suddenly, as if something had snapped inside my brain, I placed him. I thought back to the day in our kitchen before we went to The Witches Brew. I had seen his face before, although it was in black and white. He was the owner of The Witches Brew, Hansen Mills. I felt my heart quicken in response. *What were Hansen Mills and Jimmy Dickson, especially out of uniform, doing in Mrs. VanHoy's parlor?*

"Let's go, Mrs. VanHoy," I said, inching closer to the door. I tried to steady myself. "Let's go."

"Get out," said Hansen, moving closer to me. Then louder, "Get the fuck out!"

I was stunned by Hansen's aggression. I looked between Jimmy and Mrs. VanHoy. I expected one or both of them to say something, anything. Jimmy softened.

"It's okay," he said to Hansen. Then to me, "Treasure, you really should not be here. We're having a private discussion."

I did not respond to Jimmy but looked at Mrs. VanHoy.

"Let's go," I pleaded at her, tears springing to my eyes. The room blurred. I looked to the floor and tried to push down my instinct to run. I thought about

VanHoy dead in the middle of town square. I had to get her out.

"Treasure, honey, I'm fine…really," she said, but her shaky voice betrayed her. Although I knew she must be frightened, it occurred to me in that moment that she might not know that she could be in danger.

"We're leaving," I stated, my voice louder, bolder.

"You're leaving," said Hansen, now walking towards me. I could tell he was losing patience; and, as he approached, it occurred to me that he was double my size. "Get the fuck out."

Before I knew what was happening, Hansen grabbed my arm, his grip bruising. He opened the door, and tried to shove me out, but I resisted, grabbing onto one of the handles on the French door.

"Get *off* of me!!" I shrieked, losing control. He pushed back hard, and losing my balance, I fell back into the swinging door. My head smashed into the door, hard.

"Get *off* of me!" I yelled again, not recognizing my own voice.

"Treasure!" I could hear Mrs. VanHoy call. "Get off of her, Hansen!"

I heard Jimmy say something, but I could not quite make it out. I dug my nails into Hansen's red arm as I struggled to regain my balance. He grunted in response, the musky smell of stale beer filling my nostrils. My stomach lurched, and I gagged. I felt ill, sweaty, and panicked. I heard muffled scuffling in the background. My ears now ringing from the blow to my head. I kicked him in the shin, *hard*, trying desperately to get away from him. In an instant, I could feel his thick fingers groping for my neck. He pulled me up as I tried to duck and put his large, red hands around my neck, pushing into my pulse. I could not breathe.

I can't breathe! I can't breathe! was all I could think. As the air was cut off, I began to panic. I moved wildly, trying to land a blow of any kind, scratching random pieces of flesh. All I could hear was muffled shouting. Tears blurred my eyes, and I could not see. There was a crash from somewhere beyond. Right before I slipped into blackness, I caught a whiff of lavender and sage.

I awoke to the sounds of sirens. Seconds later, the police swarmed the house. A few seconds after that, we were all in handcuffs. A young officer walked me outside, and gently put me in the back of a police car. In my haze, I wondered if this would be my new memory of this house.

No longer would I look at this house and think of the magic of the Christmas party. This would be the house where I was choked and arrested. Maybe this would be the last house I would ever be in before I went to prison. I was almost too tired to care.

With each breath I took, my whole body throbbed in pain. The handcuffs cut into my wrists, and my arms, already sore, ached in their current position. Inside of the car, the smell of the air freshener, new car smell, made me feel so ill I thought I might be sick. I struggled to put my head forward, trying to put it as close to between my knees as possible, working hard to regulate my breathing.

There was a part of me that, despite being handcuffed and in the back of a police car, felt so grateful to be safe and *sitting* that I could cry. And then I did, a little. I wanted to be home, in my bed, with my mother watching over me. She would make me feel better. She would make all of this go away. As we drove the few minutes to the police station, I was so fatigued that I struggled to keep my eyes open.

Upon arriving at the police station, I was put into a small white room with just a small white table and two cold folding chairs. Thankfully, my handcuffs were removed. After what seemed like hours, an officer came in and asked if I needed to go to the hospital. I refused. I would wait here. I would die waiting here if it meant this day could be over.

Eventually, another officer, a young woman with fiery, red hair, came in and questioned me. I had never seen her before. I tried to be as calm as possible as I relayed the story to her. After she left, I waited again for what seemed like an eternity. I felt ill, as if I was drying up from the inside out. Finally, I put down my head and managed to doze off for a few minutes.

"Treasure?" A familiar voice said quietly.

I lifted my head, my neck straining in response. I could feel through my movements that a bruise was forming where Hansen's hands had been. The lump on the back of my head throbbed. I opened my eyes to see Detective Harrison. It felt so good to see his face that I began to cry. I knew I should be embarrassed, but I could not stop the tears from rolling down my face

"Jesus!" he exclaimed, scanning my face, my neck, my tears. "You okay? You wanna go to the hospital? I think you should go."

"No," I cried, unable to hold back my emotions any longer. I sobbed for a few minutes before I regained my composure, and he let me. Finally, I added, "I would like a glass of water though."

"I can get you a glass of water," he responded, kindly. Swiftly, he exited the room and returned carrying two Dixie cups filled to the brim with cold water. I sipped them slowly, hoping to settle my nerves.

"They will let you leave in just a few minutes," Harrison stated gently.

"I'm not under arrest?" I asked, trying to sound somewhat upbeat after my crying jag.

"No," he answered softly. Then smiled brightly, "Not this time."

He reached across the table slowly and put his hand on mine tentatively. His hand felt warm and reassuring. I moved my hand up, and we interlocked fingers briefly, sending jolts through my system. My body felt destroyed, yet suddenly awake again.

"I hope you put Mills away forever. That idiot Jimmy, too," I added, in a somewhat teasing tone. Only I knew that I was serious.

"Well, that is what I wanted to tell you, Treasure. While questioning Mrs. VanHoy, she confessed to murdering her husband." Harrison paused.

I was stunned.

"No! But what about the money laundering, what about," I interjected, my jaw falling open.

"I know. You were right. VanHoy was involved in money laundering with Mills. Cliff Bishop was involved as well. He was the 'muscle.' He's been working with us, as of late. Actually, he flipped on them fairly easily. VanHoy, Mills, and Bishop had some dispute over money. That is usually how it happens. Money over loyalty. I've seen it again and again. More times than I can count. Bishop and Mills are bad guys, but I do not believe they had any part in VanHoy's murder.

"Based on Mrs. VanHoy's confession, I believe we have the right person. Her story just simply makes sense. She knows things that no one else could possibly know," he said, letting out a sigh. "Sounds like she put up with a lot and just sort-of...lost it..." His voice trailed off, and he looked off into the distance.

"Sometimes, people act in ways you would never expect."

I nodded, thinking back to the article I read about his partner. I knew that people, even good people, could do things that were wrong, if pushed far enough.

"So, there you have it."

"And Jimmy?" I asked.

"I'm not sure the extent to which Jimmy was involved, but he was involved. A lot of us knew that they must have had someone helping them from the inside. I just didn't think—"

"It would be Barney Fife?" I interrupted.

He grinned genuinely now and rubbed his jaw. "No, I definitely did not think it would be Barney Fife."

"Why were Jimmy and Mills at Mrs. VanHoy's house if they are not connected to his murder?"

"We haven't quite gotten there yet, but I am assuming that they believed Mrs. VanHoy was working with law enforcement. Maybe they thought she knew something." He shrugged, "And maybe she did."

I nodded, letting it all sink in.

"So, my sisters? Deidra?"

"You are all irritating," he said with a smile. "But that's not a crime."

Exiting the police station was a long and arduous process. Numerous people came and spoke to me as I waited. Many, mercifully, brought me water and coffee. The redheaded officer from earlier offered me half a sandwich, which I readily accepted. I woofed that down in less than three bites, not even registering the type of salty lunch meat hidden inside. Finally, Chief Dodd came in.

"Well, Treasure," he said, warmly. "You are a free woman."

I smiled at him, feeling like a little kid again.

"Thank you so much. I thought I was going to have to commission some 'Free Treasure' shirts from the 'inside.'"

He laughed, "Not today, honey. Not today. Now listen, I know you've had a rough day. Please go home and take care of yourself. Call if need be. You know you girls can always call. Detective Harrison would like to walk you out. He should be here shortly."

Perfectly on cue, Harrison materialized in the doorway, looking like a detective in a sexy, *Lifetime* movie. In the movie, he would obviously be the bad guy, but would remain undiscovered to allow for several cheesy, sexy scenes between him and the protagonist. In the end, however, he would be discovered. Knife in hand, he would pursue the heroine, getting up after being knocked down beyond the point of rationality. At long last, he would be defeated. The last scene inevitably would be a depiction of a woman starting over, taking those classes, selling those paintings, or moving. All loose ends were always tied up; there was no trauma. "No mess, no fuss!" as my Aunt Elaina would say, pronouncing 'mess' like 'muss.'

The sunlight shone brightly on my face as Harrison and I exited the police station. I struggled for words to say and settled on nothing. He broke the silence first.

"Your sister Theo should be here momentarily," he explained.

Not caring about the ins-and-outs of the how she was contacted, I simply stated, "I lost my cellphone today."

He laughed softly, "That is the best thing you could have lost today."

"Well, if you find it, try not to read my text messages," I said, gently nudging him on the side. I felt comfortable with him now, in some strange way. This morning, I had hated him. But now, we had gone through battle and come out the other side, not just victorious, but allies.

"That is the first thing I will be doing," he said, looking me straight in the eye, grinning.

I wondered what this conversation even meant. Soon, I could see the familiar station wagon coming down the road and felt such a sense of relief that I almost broke down in tears again. More than anything in this world, I wanted to go home. As the car came closer, I could count three heads inside. *Of course, why wouldn't they bring the whole coven to pick up a woman from the police station? It would be absurd not to.* I began to laugh, tears streaming down my face. I should care what I looked like, but I didn't. I felt lighter somehow. *Exorcised. Released.* I had been jolted, and now I was finally awake. As I began walking to the car, Harrison called after me.

"Treasure!" he said walking briskly towards me, "There is one last thing I have to ask."

"Ok," I said, stopping and turning towards him.

"What exactly did you do to Mills?"

My face moved into a questioning expression, "What do you mean what did I do to Mills?"

Now, he looked genuinely confused. He paused for a moment.

"Well," he stated, "Whatever you did, you scared the living daylights out of him."

My expression didn't change, but Harrison nodded slightly, the left side of his mouth turning upward in a half smile. He took a few steps to the rear door of the station wagon and pulled it open for me.

"Goodbye, Treasure," he simply stated. And with that, I was safely seated in Theo's Chevrolet Caprice Classic, my mother's Chevrolet Caprice Classic, the scents of lavender and sage filling my nostrils.

Chapter 10

I suddenly realized that so many days of my life have been spent living in a silent tension. Even when seemingly at ease, I was never really at ease. Something awful lurked around every corner, and I was always 'waiting for the other shoe to drop.' *Things might seem normal now*, I would catch myself thinking, *but how many days until the next upheaval?* Maybe this could be attributed to the trauma from losing a parent—*parents*—I always seemed to forget that 'the other one' is also, in fact, my biological parent. He always seemed like a character in another person's story, my mother's story. The fact that we –Theo, Tara, and I– are his children seemed like an aside. I did not have a father. I am an extension of my mother and my aunt; I am another Culpepper woman in a long line of Culpepper women. Like a Russian doll, my mother had 'opened up' revealing three more of us. No man needed.

I usually did not allow myself space to think about my father, but I did now. I had few memories of him. But I did have some, and sometimes I could almost see his face in those memories. Like a blurry photo in my mind's eye, I would try to study the images. To my knowledge, there was not one photo of him on the property. No photos of him holding us as babies. No photos of him at one of our birthday parties. No photos of him and my mother—falling in love? Dating? Did they ever grab an ice cream cone and snap a photo? Did they ever meet for bowling night with friends? It all seemed too mundane for my mother. She was so full of life that she vibrated at a higher frequency. It was easier to imagine my mother levitating than it was to imagine her wearing bowling shoes.

As I laid in bed, I tried to conjure a memory of my father and of my father's face. Once, when I was walking to The Alchemist from school, I remembered him offering me a ride home.

"Treasure, it's me," he had said, pulling up next to me. I remember that he drove a big, shiny, black car. A big, shiny, *expensive*, black car.

"Hi," I responded, barely looking at him, watching the lines in the sidewalk as I walked.

"Get in," he said kindly. "I'll take you to the shop."

No one had ever called The Alchemist, '*the shop.*' I would not get in his car. Of course, I knew who he was; but to me, he was still a stranger. Our disconnect was never more apparent to me, even as a child, then when he called The Alchemist, '*the shop.*' At his request, I took off running.

I would lie awake sometimes, thinking about that exchange. I wondered if I was the reason that he did not want to be a father. Not just *a father*, but *my father*. Or maybe that was always the arrangement? Maybe he had no intention of ever being a father, and my mother did not want him to be. Maybe they conceptualized him as a *donor* of sorts. Still, maybe sometimes he grew curious about me and my sisters. Maybe, sometimes, he wanted to catch a glimpse of one or of all of us.

It was possible that, on that day, driving to his next location, he saw me and felt compelled to stop. Maybe I reminded him of himself. Maybe I had his nose. Or maybe I even reminded him of a distant relative he hadn't spoken to in a while. Maybe I had their eyes or their cheekbones or their exact shade of dark hair.

As an adult now, it was all so interesting to think about. You had three children wandering in the world, in the same town no less, and you weren't at least curious every once and a while? Of course, this must be why he stopped me that day. But why hadn't he stopped the thousands of other days? Bloodlines were important to the Culpepper's. But what I knew unequivocally now was that what was important to us was not always important to others.

I was still in bed from a long, restful nap. I rolled over and saw my clock realizing that I had been asleep for 3 hours. I missed the pageant; the first year in many years that I did not attend. Although it was getting late, I knew that the night was young in terms of the festivities that would be going on downtown. Things rarely wrapped up before early the following morning.

In a way, it was hard to believe this was still the same day. This was, without a doubt, the longest day of my life. On the drive home from the police station, I barely had the energy to explain what had happened. I covered the basics but was far too tired to elaborate. Too tired to go into details. Luckily, an officer had explained some things to Theo over the phone. They knew what had happened to me. What they did not know is what Harrison told me: Mrs. VanHoy confessed to killing her husband.

I did not share this fact until we arrived home. It did not seem like information you handed out while in a moving vehicle. It seemed more appropriate to tell it at home, while seated, around our things, where we could look around and see that despite this information everything was, in fact, alright. The girls' reactions to this information were unexpected. I am not sure what I was expecting: shock, denials, maybe even tears? Deidra, seated with me on the couch, pulled me into a silent hug. Theo asked just one question, *Are you sure?* Then, nodding her head, her expression blank. Tara stared at all of us, the start of a smirk on her beautiful face. She did not speak a word, but I could almost hear her thoughts, *Good. Good riddance.*

I noticed that someone had left a cup of bay-leaf tea on the table beside my bed. I sipped it slowly; it was no longer hot but was comforting all the same. If I sat very still, I could hear chatter and laughter downstairs. Listening to their happy sounds, I smiled to myself. It was time to release all this fear, this anxiety—this complacency that seemed to have a hold on me.

Everything would be okay. As bad as things had sometimes seemed, had *sometimes been*, we always ended up okay. I stirred the bay leaf inside my mug, counterclockwise. After all, I was a Culpepper. We did not bend to life. We made life bend to us.

I exited my room and began to make my way downstairs. As I descended the stairs, I was surprised to find a Halloween wonderland. While I slept, the girls had completely transformed our living room. Jack-o-lanterns sat by the roaring fireplace, their carved faces ranging from the traditional smiles to menacing open-mouth sneers. From the mantle hung a homemade garland of harvest corn, each ear tied to a thick piece of yarn. Streamers hung from the ceiling, east to west, their smooth lines occasionally broken up by a dangling papier-mâché pumpkin, black cat, or witch. On every surface, sat one of my precious candles. The scent of pumpkin—earthy, spicy, and sweet—hung in the air.

I swung open the kitchen door to find Theo, Tara, Deidra, and, to my surprise, Ronnie, sitting around the kitchen counter carving more pumpkins.

"Should we yell surprise?" asked Tara with a snicker, as she saw me enter.

"Surprise!" Deidra yelled half-heartedly, taking a pause from her work, a smile on her face.

"The house looks great!" I exclaimed. "Just like Mom and Aunt Elaina used to do it!"

"Exactly," Theo said. She stood up from her stool, grabbed a thick wool blanket, and hugged it around my shoulders. "Exactly."

I quickly realized that while I slept not only had they transformed the house, but the girls had whipped up a feast that was a celebration all its own. It included a thick beef stew stuffed with potatoes, carrots, and rosemary, a blackberry cobbler with a thick layer of cinnamon-sugar oatmeal crust, pumpkin bread topped with chopped walnuts, and even homemade biscuits dripped with honey. It was not long before all abandoned their pumpkins to settle in at the dining room table. Sharing a bottle of cranberry wine, we all gorged ourselves until we were absolutely stuffed.

"I think I've gained at least 10 pounds since I started hanging out with you guys," Ronnie said, patting his stomach. "Thank you all so much for allowing me to join in and for...you know...feeding me."

"Of course, Ronnie! You know you are welcome here anytime," Theo said, enthusiastically.

Tara rolled her eyes at Theo's enthusiasm.

"Call first though," Tara retorted with a smile patting Ronnie on the arm. "Best to call first."

We all laughed; Ronnie's face turned a bit pink.

"Well, what now?" asked Deidra, after the last drop of wine had been poured.

"Should we all 'go party'?" I asked, feeling invigorated, like I could conquer anything.

"What?" asked Theo, turning to me, shocked. "You really want to go downtown after everything you've been through today?"

"Yes!" I exclaimed with a laugh. "I really do!"

"Let's do it!" cried Tara.

"Ok, we're doing this," Deidra said, nodding her head happily.

"I'm in!" declared Ronnie.

We all turned to look at Theo, who seemed contemplative.

When she finally spoke, she said, "Ok, fine, but we're definitely calling a car!"

It took all of us girls just 15 minutes to get ready. Deidra hopped from room to room, trying on clothes and eyeing different shades of lipstick before picking a deep shade of purple.

"To hide the cranberry wine stains!" she said with a laugh, puckering her lips out to show us the burgundy tint.

Then, we all piled into our Uber, Tara sitting across Theo's and my lap. I looked over at Ronnie and smiled, a little embarrassed by our proximity. I wondered how he got here. Did he come to talk to me? Check on me? Or was he merely 'stopping by.' Of course, I had to wonder, who just stopped by the Culpepper estate.

As expected, downtown was still incredibly busy. The car dropped us off right at the town square, where we all exited, with Ronnie helping each of us out. The spider gazebo looked incredible in the moonlight. Inside, many tables and chairs had been removed to make a dance floor. A DJ booth stood in one corner of the structure on a folding table, with a garland that read "Happy All Hallows Eve Seven Hills" across the front. A vaguely familiar Top-40 hit blasted from the speakers.

We all stood on the edge of the dance floor, watching for a few minutes. It was clear that most people were heavily intoxicated from a long day of partaking in the festivities. At one point, a strange man, wearing a Hawaiian shirt with jack-o-lanterns on it, tried to get Tara to dance. I could not hear her response, but I knew it had to be some sort of rejection as the man made a sad face, shrugged, turned, and danced away.

"Are you going to dance?" I asked Ronnie, yelling over the music.

"No! Of course not," he grinned, learning towards me, obviously amused at the spectacle. "First of all, I'm afraid of looking like 'that guy,'" he said as he pointed to the recently rejected gentleman in the pumpkin-Hawaiian, chic attire. Then, he added, "Also, all I need is for a student to see me and put that on *YouTube*. You go, though. I'll get us some drinks."

"Actually," I replied, "I'll go with you. I don't need 'that guy' in my life."

We made our way through the gazebo to the outdoor cash bar, where we bought 5 beers, and donated to the Seven Hills Rotary Club.

"So, I am assuming that the girls told you what happened?" I asked tentatively, when we were far enough away to prevent the people at the bar from overhearing us, and far enough away from the DJ booth to hear each other.

"Yes. I am really glad you are okay."

"And about Mrs. VanHoy?"

"Yes, they filled me in on that as well. I never thought of that one. Although, based on what I know from the data, I should have. As a researcher, I should never make assumptions based on my own experiences or opinions."

He looked so thoughtful that I had to laugh.

"Well, it is harder to see things when it is 'close to home,'" I interjected. *I should know.*

"Well, either way, VanHoy, Mills, and Cliff are all clearly criminals, even if they are not murderers. I'm glad all of this is coming to light. I'm just sorry it had to be at your expense and at the expense of your sisters and Deidra."

"Yes," I nodded. "But I think it has been good for me, in a way."

"What do you mean?"

"I've learned I have some things to figure out about myself. I feel like I can do that now," I explained.

Ronnie nodded. He seemed unsure of what to say or what move to make next. He opened his mouth, as if to speak, and then closed it again.

"Maybe you could help me," I offered. "Help me fill in the blanks when it comes to my family, my family history. I could pay you...in food...or love potions...or something."

He laughed softly, "Love potions? I could use one of those."

"Oh really?" I questioned, giving him an over-exaggerated shocked face.

"I would give anything to see you create or use a love potion."

Ronnie chuckled, "Am I really that...ah hem...square?"

"No," I grinned. "Just academic."

His voice turned a little serious when he replied, "I'm other things too, you know."

We looked at each other straight in the eyes then.

"I can see that," I responded, taking his hand and squeezing it. And I could.

"Ok, it's a deal then," I replied, reluctantly letting go of his hand. "Now, let's get back to the girls. They'll wonder where we ran off to."

Inside the gazebo, Theo had procured a table with five chairs. Ronnie sat down with Theo and our beers. Tara and Deidra, on the dance floor, saw me and motioned for me to join them. I set down my bag near Theo and made a beeline towards them, the music thumping loudly in my ears. I imaged the noise cleansing me, removing all my fears and doubts. Sound, I knew, was a powerful tool. Tara and Deidra laughed at me, as I was having an almost spiritual experience on the dance floor.

Eventually, they joined in my dancing, all of us moving wildly. I imagined all my ancestors dancing with their sisters, whether biological or chosen, on this sacred night, absorbing all that nature had to offer. Despite the fact that the temperature had dropped since earlier in the day, sweat began to bead on my forehead and run down my sides.

"I'm going to get some water!" I yelled over the music to Tara and Deidra, neither of whom seemed to notice or miss a beat.

I emerged from the gazebo into the moonlight. The cool air hit my damp skin, making me shiver. I walked away from the crowd, my eyes still on the moon. It was a waning moon, a perfect moon for letting go. I suddenly wished for the solace of home so that I could pay my respects to the universe for protecting me and my family.

"I can't believe you'd come back down here after the day you've had," Harrison's voice said. I jumped, unaware I was not alone. I whirled around to see Harrison walking towards me.

"What are you doing here?" I questioned. He was the last person I expected to see here. He was still dressed as he was earlier. I imagined that he probably just left the police station.

"Can't a man come enjoy the festivities?" he asked.

"I didn't know you were into All Hallows' Eve. Anyway, I thought this town 'stressed you out'," I teased, looking straight into his clear blue eyes. I smiled at him.

He smiled back. "Well, in all fairness, it was less about the town and more about *you*."

"For a man that finds my presence so stressful, you sure find ways to be around me...a lot," I stated, deadpan. The wine, the dancing, and maybe even the near-death experience made me bolder.

He threw his head back and laughed, his white, square teeth sparkling in the moonlight.

"How do you know I didn't think you were the murderer?" he asked, teasingly.

"Well, did you?" I asked, cocking my head to the side waiting for his answer.

"Naw, I didn't think you could pull off something like that," he mocked. "But now, I'm wondering what you *can* pull off." He lowered his voice with the last sentence. He seemed almost like he was talking to, almost questioning, himself.

"I guess you'll never know," I stated. "I assume you're leaving now that the case is solved."

"You won't get rid of me that easily," he replied. "I plan to stay put for a while. There are some loose ends that need to be tied up on some cases."

I swallowed, *what cases?*

As if sensing my thoughts, he explained, "On the money laundering case, specifically."

I wondered if he had looked into other cold cases. There had to be information on my biological father's disappearance, some files in a drawer somewhere collecting dust. I wish I could look at those files. But if I did, what information would I find, and would I really want to know?

I nodded and adjusted my shoulders, "Just let me know if you need any help, Detective."

He chuckled again, lightening the mood, "You know what? I think I'm good. But, I will call you if I need to scare off any bad guys."

"Scaring off men is my specialty," I remarked, still not sure how I scared Mills so badly. He assaulted *me*. I was half of his size. *How did I frighten him?*

"That I can't believe. I see you spending a lot of time with the professor," he replied.

"We're friends," I replied quickly. "...Despite what Kristy Pickles might have told you."

"Ah. She is interesting, isn't she? She's filled me in on a lot. But, I've personally seen you and Professor Jackman together. Also, in her defense, I asked about you," he revealed. "Not that she needed encouragement."

"Ah," I nodded. "In an official capacity?"

"Totally off the record," he countered, his eyes never leaving mine.

My stomach flipped, and I broke our eye contact first.

"Well great, now there will be rumors about us," I muttered, but smiled unwillingly.

"Hope so," Harrison responded, raising his eyebrows, and revealing that stunning smile. "You know...it might ingratiate me with the locals."

Now, it was my turn to throw my head back and howl.

"Wow. You call yourself a detective? Aren't *you* the one who told us the local police department was ready to round up my whole family? You think association with *us* is going to win you favor? You *do* need my help to put things together, don't you?"

He laughed again, warmly, like we were old friends.

"I should be going. I haven't had much time for sleep lately. I'll see you again?" he asked.

"I'm sure you will. I'm sure you will."

He looked at me again, intently, and gave a slight nod, "I look forward to it."

As I made my way back to the gazebo, I wondered if he meant what he said.

Back inside, the whole crew was seated at the table. They all looked, as my Aunt Elaina would have said, *beat*. I had barely consulted a mirror before we left and wondered if the day was written all over my own face as well.

"Where were you?" Deidra asked.

"Getting air," I answered. "Just getting some air."

"Are you ready to go?" asked Theo. "I think we are all exhausted."

I nodded. I was ready to go. Time for this day to end. We exited the gazebo. Before we parted ways, each of us gave Ronnie a hug. We lingered, making small talk, before watching him crawl into the back of an Uber. We did the same with Deidra, promising her that we would call if we needed anything at all. Theo, Tara, and I climbed into the back of our Uber after both had left. On the way home, we were quiet, fatigue catching up with all of us.

"I'm exhausted!" Tara declared, flinging herself onto the sofa upon reentering our home.

Theo turned and locked the door.

"Me too," she responded moving to the seating area and sliding into a chair.

"The longest day ever," I said with a smile, also plopping down in an easy chair.

"You really doing okay?" Theo asked. I noticed Tara was struggling to keep her eyes open.

"I really am," I responded. "I really am."

"I honestly just can't believe that Mrs. VanHoy did that. *Could do that*," Theo said shaking her head.

Tara sat up straight now, looking straight ahead. I could not tell if she was deep in thought or so tired that she could not move.

"I know," I admitted. "It just does not seem like her...like the woman we know."

"I'm not surprised," Tara interjected.

"You're not?" Theo asked, incredulous.

"No," Tara responded assuredly. "It's the wife. It's always the wife."

I shuddered, remembering Sarah Tarleton, in my dream, telling me the same thing. *The wife did it*, she told me, *the wife did it*. Ronnie said it in so many words himself. *As a researcher, I should never make assumptions based on my own experiences or opinions.* The words echoed in my head. They were right. They had to be. It was always the wife.

We all looked at each other.

"Holy shit," Theo murmured.

About The Authors

Keri

Keri Kovacsiss is an instructor of sociology at a college in Ohio. She attended Heidelberg University (2010) and the University of Toledo (2013). *Just Beneath the Surface* was inspired by her love for Halloween and all things cozy. You can find Keri hiking, reading anything and everything about the occult, decorating for Halloween long before it is socially acceptable, and spending time with her husband, Ryan, and their dog, Pumpkin.

Lea

Lea Kovacsiss works in law enforcement as a research specialist in Ohio. She attended Tiffin University (2006; 2007) and Alliant International University (2011), where she earned her Ph.D. *Just Beneath the Surface* was the perfect opportunity to channel her vast knowledge of homicide and law enforcement into something more appropriate for polite conversation. You can find Lea baking and hosting dinner parties for family and friends.

Made in the USA
Monee, IL
25 August 2022

11519955R10134